"I found freedom and peace in that cove for a few minutes of relaxation—"

"—and then I entered the picture and everything went to hell," Claire inserted doggedly.

"I have not a single regret about what happened between us," Raif told her with conviction. "It was the most real connection I have ever enjoyed with a woman. Why would I wish that we had never met at all?"

"You'll regret it deeply once I tell you what I have to tell you," Claire warned him tautly.

Raif frowned as he lifted his tea from the tray. "So, talk..."

"I've done a test and I'm pregnant," Claire informed him quietly.

He set down the tea with a jarring rattle of china. "Are you sure of this?"

"The test was positive."

Lynne Graham was born in Northern Ireland and has been a keen romance reader since her teens. She is very happily married to an understanding husband who has learned to cook since she started to write! Her five children keep her on her toes. She has a very large dog who knocks everything over, a very small terrier who barks a lot and two cats. When time allows, Lynne is a keen gardener.

Books by Lynne Graham

Harlequin Presents

The Ring the Spaniard Gave Her
The Italian's Bride Worth Billions

Heirs for Royal Brothers

Cinderella's Desert Baby Bombshell
Her Best Kept Royal Secret

The Stefanos Legacy

Promoted to the Greek's Wife
The Heirs His Housekeeper Carried
The King's Christmas Heir

Visit the Author Profile page
at Harlequin.com for more titles.

Lynne Graham

THE BABY THE DESERT KING MUST CLAIM

HARLEQUIN
PRESENTS

HARLEQUIN®
PRESENTS™

ISBN-13: 978-1-335-58426-7

Recycling programs
for this product may
not exist in your area.

The Baby the Desert King Must Claim

For questions and comments about the quality of this book,
please contact us at CustomerService@Harlequin.com.

Harlequin Enterprises ULC
22 Adelaide St. West, 41st Floor
Toronto, Ontario M5H 4E3, Canada
www.Harlequin.com

Printed in U.S.A.

THE BABY THE DESERT
KING MUST CLAIM

CHAPTER ONE

EVEN ANCHORED OUT in the bay, the mega yacht, *Mahnoor*, towered above every other craft moored at the marina of the Greek island of Kanos, including the local ferry. For all its size and the looming tiers of deck, however, the slick lines of the pristine vessel had been designed for speed and elegance.

From the shelter of the top-deck office, the owner, Prince Raif Sultan bin Al-Rashid, better known in the business world as the billionaire resort and property developer, Raif Sultan, was receiving a pre-arranged call from his royal father, King Jafri of Quristan. What on earth could the father who had virtually ignored him since his birth want from him? Only seconds into the awkward opening dialogue, Raif found out and it wasn't pleasant.

'You have signed a contract to build a

town *and* a resort on Quristani land,' his father hissed. 'You will tear it up and forget about the idea!'

Raif bristled. 'It has the government's support.'

'It does not have mine!' the older man exclaimed. 'I do not want tourists in my country.'

'I can only be sorry for that,' Raif countered stiffly. 'The new port and luxury resort would bring a lot of employment to a poor area. All conservation advice will be respected in the development and the resort will have the minimum possible impact on the natural habitat.'

'I have told you how I feel. That should be sufficient to change your mind,' the older man interrupted in another burst of outrage.

'I cannot pull out of a contract that has already been signed and approved by the government,' Raif responded wryly.

'I will not call you my son again if you disobey me,' King Jafri cut in fiercely. 'Obeying me is your primary duty as my son and I will not tolerate your disobedience!'

The phone went crashing down in Quristan. Raif breathed in slowly and carefully and then swore long and low in English. His duty? *His duty?* Was he a child to be told what to do and how to do it? And by a man whom he barely knew? A man who had never once acted like a father to him? A man who had never made a personal call to him in his life before? Nor granted him a single one-to-one meeting?

Unlike his two much older brothers, Hashir and Waleed, Raif had grown up in the UK. His brothers were the heir and spare to the monarchy of Quristan and had grown up there, separated from Raif and his mother. The King's third son had become an irrelevant extra after his father had said goodbye to him and his ex-wife when Raif was still a baby. Possibly guilt over the divorce and the damage that that divorce had inflicted on the former Queen's mental health had ensured that his father had turned his back on both ex-wife and third son, because the older man had taken little further interest in Raif's development. Aside of the royal summons Raif would receive to attend occasional ceremonial events in his birth country, it seemed that Raif was surplus to his father's requirements.

Pure rage now roared through Raif as he recovered from the shock of his domineering royal parent's demands and his lean hands knotted into fists. He recognised the pain of rejection laced through that rage and that only made him angrier. He was twenty-seven years old, no longer a child desperate for his father's attention. He should be long past such weak feelings. He had survived without his father's regard and had learned to value his own achievements.

He had realised that he had to stand on his own feet at twenty-one, when, after his obligatory year's national service in the Quristani army, he had opted to leave soldiering behind him and return to the business world. His father hadn't approved of that move either. He would have preferred a career soldier for a third son. Raif had merely reminded himself that neither of his older brothers had even managed to complete that single year's service. Hashir had dropped out with a minor ankle injury and Waleed had used a weak stomach as an excuse to evade the army altogether.

In a volatile mood, he left his office to stride down the companionway and leave the yacht. He needed fresh air and activity. He stepped into the waiting speedboat, only to frown when a surge of security staff rushed in after him. He wanted to be alone. He wanted the freedom to scream to the skies if he wanted to. What did he need with a protection team on a sleepy Greek island he barely remembered the name of? There were no tourists around, no paparazzi, nobody to arouse concern.

'But, Your Highness, we must keep you safe.' At the Quristani government's insistence, the crack Special Forces guard imposed on him protested while his private security team stood back.

'I only want to go for a walk,' Raif breathed tautly.

'Danger lurks in unexpected places,' Mohsin told him worriedly.

'Watch me from a distance,' Raif urged wearily, worn down by that intensity focussed on his safety.

Aware that he was poorly dressed for such an outing because he was wearing a business suit, Raif stepped out onto the quay, the warmth of the sun beating down on him, but it was no challenge for a man accustomed to the scorching heat of the desert.

He had spent every summer in Quristan, wandering the sands with his uncle's nomadic tribe in Rabalissa. His mother had been the Queen of Rabalissa before she married his father and united the two countries. It had been a very popular alliance. Rabalissa was small and backward and Quristan was large and oil rich. Sadly, in spite of his late mother's hopes, Rabalissa had profited very little from that marriage and the current government was keen to redress that inequality. Unfortunately, his father was too rigid in his views to acknowledge the poverty and dissatisfaction creating unrest in the area.

Striding away from the harbour, Raif chose to follow a worn track out of the village that followed the coastline. Only briefly did he consider contacting his brothers for advice and he quickly discarded the idea. From what he had witnessed from afar over the years, his older brothers managed their father by never ever disagreeing with him, no matter how unreasonable he was. But surely even the King had to recognise that a

legal contract could not be set aside once it
was signed? Raif breathed out in exasperation, his pace picking up as he strode below
the trees. Frustration currented through him
because he realised that the vast development project would now be beset by every
stumbling block his father could find to
throw in its path.

As the path dipped into a small, secluded
cove, Raif crossed the sand. He wrenched
his tie loose, tugging it off to put it in the
pocket of his jacket. The blue-green water
looked so inviting and he was getting warm.
It was peaceful being alone and he didn't get
to be alone often enough, he conceded ruefully. Well, he no longer felt like screaming
to the skies, but he did feel like getting into
the water to cool off.

From below the shade of the tree sheltering
her from the sun, Claire was taking a video
of the gorgeous view for the benefit of Lottie, her friend back in London. When a man
in a suit appeared in the lens, she frowned in
bemusement because he was such an incon-
gruous sight. Nobody got dressed up on the
island unless there was a wedding or a fu-

neral but, come to think of it, she reflected, she had seen flowers being carried into the village church, so he could well be a guest. He peeled off his jacket and set it down on a rock and then removed his shirt. So, he was going in for a swim, she assumed, watching him haul off the shirt to reveal a muscular golden torso straight out of a superhero movie.

At that point, Claire was transfixed, peering into her phone, intent on the sight. He was very tall and black-haired, and he was indisputably incredibly well built. It had been longer than she liked to admit since she had seen such a very attractive man because most of the islanders were middle-aged or elderly. He tossed off shoes and socks and peeled off the narrow-cut trousers to reveal what she assumed to be boxers, rather than swim shorts. However, at that point, she got a little uncomfortable and decided that if the boxers came off as well, she should stop filming and look away. But without hesitation he turned and walked into the sea, long, powerful, hair-roughened legs ploughing through the surf.

He was a strong swimmer as well, bowling through the currents near the rocks that made her nervous. With a sigh, Claire stopped filming and sent the clip off for Lottie's enjoyment. At least it would give her friend a wicked giggle.

'You're the only person I know who's spent over six months in Greece and hasn't even picked up a boyfriend,' Lottie had lamented during their most recent chat. 'I'm a mum, a wife and an employee in a very boring job. I need some titillation.'

A boyfriend was the last thing she needed, Claire thought ruefully, although since her mother's demise, she had felt agonisingly lonely and isolated. The past tumultuous ten months had been a time of confusion and emotional turmoil but ultimately a kind of renewal even though she had been left sad and alone. She had learned so much about herself, yet everything she had once believed she knew about her parentage had been thrown up in the air and the pattern of the truth had proved startlingly different once all the pieces had settled back into place. It had all begun when she had been clearing her father's desk out after his death...

'I'm sorry, I didn't realise that there was

anyone here,' a rather correct English masculine drawl imparted.

Claire emerged from her reverie and went
rather hot in the face as she looked up and
saw the man who had strayed into her video
of the bay, standing only a few feet away. He
was holding his clothes in a bundle in front of
him. And close up he was the best-looking guy
she had seen in her entire life, so excitingly,
wickedly hot he was literally off-the-scale perfection. Fine ebony brows slashed over dark
golden eyes that were deep set, rimmed with
dense black lashes and frankly stunning. Add
in a refined bone structure, cheekbones like
blades, a classic nose and a wide full mouth
and he just about took her breath away.

'I hope I didn't disturb you,' he completed,
studying her with an intent gaze, because she
was an outrageously pretty woman with long,
silky corn-gold hair sliding round her shoulders, big blue eyes and a scattering of freckles.

'No, but you gave me a great video clip,'
she told him with a radiant smile. 'I was
filming the cove and I wasn't expecting a
man to walk into view and do a strip for me.'

'You filmed me...*undressed*?' Raif
breathed in shock, because that was not the

kind of thing he could afford to have float-
ing about the Internet. Although he had
grown up in a very different world, he tried
to honour the very conservative mores of his
Quristani family as best he could.

'It's not as though you were naked!' Claire
declared, picking up on his discomfiture
and colouring over the suspicion that he
believed that she had done something that
she shouldn't have done. 'It's a public beach.
People take off their clothes to go swim-
ming. It's no big deal.'

'I must ask you out of courtesy to delete
it from your camera.'

Claire froze and noted the grim hold he
had on his clothes. In a sudden move she
pulled out the towel she had used as a pad at
her back and extended it to him. 'Here. You
might as well get dressed while we argue.'

'Thank you. I have no intention of having an argument with you,' Raif told her
smoothly, accepting the towel and walking
away to turn his back on her to towel himself
dry and dress. He was kind of cautious and
almost shy for a guy who looked as though
he would be a complete extrovert. His rock-
solid confidence and sophistication had been

dazzlingly obvious until she'd made the mistake of mentioning the video clip.

Disconcerted by that jarring contrast, Claire shook her head slightly as though to clear it and watched the long golden muscles of his back flex, her face warming again. He was somehow like chocolate when she was on a diet. He had an irresistible allure she had never seen in a man before. One look didn't cut it. She would keep on looking as long as she could. Instant attraction, she supposed. That was a new experience for her.

He walked back towards her, all lean and long and golden with still damp black hair. He looked amazing. 'Look, let me buy your phone from you and replace it because I am inconveniencing you,' he suggested levelly.

'Let's not get silly about something so trivial,' Claire urged in dismay as voices sounded on the path above them.

'Are you on holiday here?' he enquired.

'No. I've been living here for a while but I'm planning to return to the UK.' Her voice trailed off because she wouldn't be doing that until she had saved up enough for the flight home and had sufficient cash to put towards accommodation. Her decision to

stay in Greece with her late mother had left
her pretty much penniless but she had no
regrets about the sacrifices she had made.

A bunch of local children with a lone
adult in tow flooded the beach with whoops
and cries and a football. As her companion
returned the towel to her with an air of reluctance, Claire gave him an uneasy smile.
She stood up, gathering her book, and hesitated before deciding to be honest. 'There
would be no point in deleting that clip from
my phone. I've already sent it on to a friend.
I will, naturally, ask her to ensure that she
doesn't share it with anyone else and I doubt
if she will. I'm afraid that's the best I can
offer...*oomph*!' She gasped as the football
struck her squarely in the solar plexus and
knocked her off balance.

She almost contrived to right herself and
then she fell, glancing off the rocks below
her into the sand, striking one leg painfully
on the rough surface.

She was instantly the centre of attention
and it was the sort of fuss Claire hated. The
adult rushed over to apologise and to ask
if she was all right. Her male companion
lifted her out of the sand in silence and ex-

pressively eyed the blood running from the abrasion on her knee. He addressed the little footballer in a censorious tone as the boy bleated out fervent apologies. He was the son of Claire's landlord, a nice child, and she was quick to assure him that accidents happened and that she was fine.

'But you're *not*…fine,' the man beside her pronounced.

'I'll survive!' Claire hissed up at him, intimidated by the sheer height of him now that they were standing level. She was exactly five feet tall and he topped her by more than a foot.

'You have been *hurt*,' he continued with concern.

And in truth she had been. She had bashed her leg and her hip, and both were aching, while her knee was stinging like mad, but she had no intention of parading either her bruises or her wound. She flung him an upward glance that heavily suggested he stay silent. 'I'm on my way home anyway,' she announced brightly in the hope that the crowd of interested onlookers around her would lose interest.

'Where do you live?'

'Only a few yards up the hill. You can't

see the house because of the trees. This cove is almost my front garden,' she joked, wincing as she moved up the beach.

'I'll see you back to your home,' he insisted.

'It's not necessary.'

He gave her a look of unapologetic disagreement. Heavens, those tortoiseshell eyes practically talked, she thought in a daze as they both moved up the steep path to the small house behind the trees where her mother had lived for years.

'Are you in the habit of taking pictures of random strangers taking off their clothes?'

'Why are you making me sound like some pervert?' Claire gasped in horror. 'It's a public beach. If you're so precious about your privacy, why did you undress there?'

'I was thoughtless. I believed I was alone. I was enjoying that sensation. I wasn't trying to make you feel like a pervert. I was simply trying to understand what made you do such a peculiar thing.'

'Well, you wandered into the viewing lens, and I saw you, and I sort of stared without thinking about what I was doing...' Claire snatched in a ragged breath because the hill had a stiff gradient and she was embarrassed. 'And I thought… I thought—'

'You thought what?' he sliced in impatiently, his tension palpable in his wary appraisal. 'That you recognised me from somewhere?'

Claire stopped dead outside the low-built house. 'No, why would I have? I thought you were beautiful. No harm in that, is there?'

Raif eyed her burning face. 'Beautiful?' he repeated incredulously. 'Men aren't *beautiful*.'

'Don't be sexist.' Claire stiffened her shoulders, wondering why she had mortified herself with that admission, but he was as relentless as a train roaring down a track at speed. When he had a goal in view, he couldn't be headed off.

'So, you're saying it was lust,' Raif gathered with a sudden flashing wicked grin.

'No, I wasn't saying that at all. I just admired you for a few seconds.'

'While I took my clothes off. If you were a man, you would surely be arrested for such an invasion of privacy,' Raif quipped, starting to enjoy himself in a way he rarely did in female company. He could not credit that she was a member of the paparazzi tribe or

that she had the smallest clue who he was.
Her lack of tact and inability to dissemble
were phenomenal.

'It wasn't *lust*,' Claire repeated with
dignity. 'I can admire a painting without
needing to own it, but I will agree it was
thoughtless of me not to consider your feelings…although most of the men I've met
aren't quite so modest and would be quite
flattered by admiration. You're in a class of
your own, it seems.'

'Very much so,' he confirmed with another
slanting grin as he paused by the outside table
and chairs. 'Now, sit down. Have you a first-
aid kit? Your knee needs attention.'

'What's your name?' she demanded
abruptly, quite dizzy in the radius of that
charming smile of amusement.

'Raif…' he told her. 'Although it sounds
the same as the English name Rafe, it is spelt
differently.'

'I'm Claire. It was my mother's favourite
name and she's gone now,' she told him,
pushing open the back door and disappear-
ing inside. 'Would you like a cold drink?
I have a jug of lemonade in the fridge. It's
very refreshing.'

'Bring out the first-aid kit first.'

'No, the first thing I'm going to do,' she said, walking back to the door to look out at him with sparkling blue eyes in which mischief danced as bright as stardust, 'is warn my friend that she must on *no* account show that clip to anyone else. I will also ask her to delete it.'

'At the same time as you delete your own version,' Raif incised.

'Oh, must I?' Claire teased him, helpless to resist that temptation. 'If you're my object of lust, won't I be wanting to keep it and savour it on dark lonely nights?'

Raif laughed out loud. Her ready tongue and her liveliness were extraordinarily appealing. He had never been a womaniser; in fact, he saw himself as being of a sombre, serious disposition and he definitely didn't know how to flirt. Growing up with a depressed and suicidal mother, while striving to tolerate the promiscuous lifestyle that had eventually become her sole consolation, had matured Raif much faster than his peers. After divorce had destroyed Mahnoor's life by depriving her of the husband she loved, her two elder sons and the royal role she had cherished, his mother had only had Raif to sustain her. Her chaotic private life had put him off casual sex and everything that went with it.

Yet he was no longer so sure of the rigid decisions he had reached when he was younger because, for literally the first time, Raif was very much tempted by a woman. Claire was small and curvy and full of personality, the complete opposite of the polished, socially repressed young women he usually met, who calculated every expression and every word in his radius. Claire didn't know he was wealthy and, what was more, he suspected that even if she did she wouldn't be impressed by the superficial show of his material possessions.

'First-aid kit,' he reminded her, having already noticed in some exasperation that she drifted and darted from topic to topic like a colourful hummingbird sipping from flowers, finding each as alluring as the previous one.

'And lemonade?'

'Why not?' Raif said easily, following her indoors to a tiny galley kitchen, suspecting that he would have to find the first-aid kit for himself while she poured lemonade and chattered.

'I suppose I should have offered you a beer.'

'I don't drink.'

'Neither do I,' she confided cheerfully. 'But I keep some beer for a friend who calls in occasionally.'

'A man?' For some reason, Raif found himself tensing at that idea.

Claire pulled a face. 'Good heavens, no. It's a small island and it wouldn't do to get the neighbours talking. My friend, Sofia. I work with her sometimes down at the harbour bar.'

Relieved by the explanation, Raif found the first-aid kit shoved in a corner and clicked it open to find it empty, which didn't surprise him. Claire opened a drawer and rustled madly through the cluttered interior to produce plasters and medicated ointment, passing him kitchen towelling on demand and dampening a piece for him. 'I'll do it,' she told him as she poured the lemonade and lifted the glasses to pass him one. 'But I warn you, I'll probably scream if it hurts. I'm not that brave.'

'Sit down,' he told her as he set aside the glass.

'There's no seats in here.'

'If you will allow me...' Raif extended his arms. 'I will set you on the counter.'

Claire laughed. 'If you like, but I'm no Skinny Minnie... Mind you, you do have all those muscles I was insensitive enough to admire.'

Laughing, Raif scooped her up and found her even lighter than he had expected. Blonde hair that had a lemony scent brushed his jaw and flared his nostrils, unleashing a vibrant awareness of her femininity. A heaviness settled in his groin. He settled her down gently and turned his attention to her knee, cleaning the cut with tiny careful movements, frowning over the sand he had to remove, impossibly conscious of her every wince but, apart from the occasional flinch, she didn't make a sound. 'It's bruising and it will scar,' he warned her.

'I'll survive,' she told him buoyantly as he used the ointment and fixed on an adhesive plaster. 'To be honest, I'm going to have more than a few bruises from that fall.'

'You insisted that you were fine.'

'I didn't want to upset Dimitris. He's a good kid. Accidents happen.'

'Not if due care is exercised.'

'You sound like you swallowed a health and safety manual,' Claire reproved.

After a disconcerted pause, Raif straightened and laughed with genuine appreciation of that criticism. That kind of impertinence rarely came his way. 'Boring, you mean?' he chided.

'A little set in your ways. I bet you were raised as a child to be seen and not heard. I know I was. My father believed an outspoken child was the devil's work,' she confided ruefully. 'He was very strict.'

The rules of the royal nursery even under his adoring mother's sway had been hard and harsh, not least because his father had insisted on a strict nanny for his youngest son. 'So, you rebelled,' he assumed, lifting his hands to her waist to lift her down again.

'Not when I was a kid. I was too hooked on wanting my father's approval,' Claire admitted ruefully, one flimsy flip-flop falling off as he set her down. She lurched against him to steady herself, her hands flying out to clutch at his jacket.

She looked up into smouldering dark golden eyes, her heart beating so fast it felt as though it were in her throat. It was one of those out-of-time moments, freezing her there as this great wave of yearning surged through her. She couldn't look away from his eyes and as his head came down she stretched up, her breath parting her lips. She had never wanted a kiss so badly.

'Kiss me,' she urged, helpless in the grip of that powerful craving.

And Raif unfroze at the invitation, insanely aware of his arousal and the sheer temptation of those soft luscious lips. He shook off the discipline of years with an unfamiliar feeling of daring, of resentment for all the times he had stepped back from women, always telling himself that he was living up to his ideals. For what reason? For what ultimate purpose? he questioned now.

He drew her up to him with slow, careful hands, brushed his mouth very softly across hers and then doubled back to steal a fierce, hungry kiss. His tongue eased in, plundered, tasted, taking everything and more that she offered, his lean, powerful body thrumming with all the raw, flaring excitement he had always restrained. But there was something about her, something about Claire that made that restraint impossible.

Claire emerged trembling and perspiring

from that passionate kiss. She had been waiting a long time to feel that passion with a guy and she was shaken by suddenly finding it. So great was the shock that she stepped back from him, immediately denying that unexpected bond. And she thought of letting him go, indeed showing him to the door for daring to tempt her to that extent. But just as quickly came the need to explore that sense of connection and discover if it was only an illusion.

'Stay for supper,' she told him instead, backing away, flushed and bemused by what he had made her feel and yet unable to send him away.

Raif hovered, unbearably aroused, fighting for control—for the cool that was usually his with a woman. Supper? *Food?* The suggestion that he stay longer? He was fully on board with that idea when he didn't want to leave her.

'Why not?' he responded, grateful for the jacket that concealed his arousal, striving to remain cool in spite of the embarrassing truth that he was deeply out of his depth. His phone thrummed silently in his pocket and he clenched his teeth. His security team?

'Excuse me,' he murmured softly. 'I must take this call.'

Claire watched him step outside and pull out a phone, but she was infinitely more interested in that moment about what she planned to feed him.

Raif stepped out onto the terrace, which was paved but full of weeds, and studied the clutch of bodyguards stationed at the bottom corner of the small front garden under the trees with raised brows and irritation.

'Sir?' Mohsin queried. 'You are in a strange house.'

Raif grinned. He wanted to laugh. His security team were not accustomed to him deviating from the norm. He was breaking out of his expected routine and they were nervous, concerned by his behaviour.

'I am fine. I am staying here and… I may be late back.' He framed that prospect stiffly. 'I will return to the harbour when I am ready. There is no need to remain here on guard.'

And that was the instant that Raif appreciated that he had reached a decision. He was done with control and restraint, ready to run a risk for the first time ever.

CHAPTER TWO

'GO AND RELAX in the sitting room,' Claire advised when he reappeared. 'I'll be busy in the kitchen.'

Resisting the ridiculous temptation to admit that he only wanted her to be busy with him, Raif strode into a tiny room ornamented with plants, books tumbled on the floor and a window seat on which a very elegant black cat posed. Claire followed him in. 'This is Circe,' she told him. 'Don't worry if she ignores you. She's very fussy about who she likes. I really had to work at impressing her when I first arrived.'

'And when was that? When did you first come to Greece?'

Claire froze on the way back into the kitchen. 'Ten months ago. I came to the island to meet my mother...and I ended up staying here,' she confided reluctantly.

'Sounds like a story. Meet her…for the *first* time?' Raif stressed in surprise.

Claire nodded. 'She left my father and me when I was still a baby.'

Raif frowned.

'It's not as bad as it sounds,' Claire proclaimed defensively on her mother's behalf. 'I grew up being told what a wicked woman she was. I was about four when my stepmother told me that my mother was a bad person and that I had to be careful not to grow up to be like her.'

'That must have been challenging,' Raif remarked, utterly enchanted by her honesty and the less than perfect background that she was revealing. People literally *never* made him the recipient of such revelations. He was as hooked on her outspokenness as someone exposed for the first time to fresh air. He had often felt that he was the only person he knew who had grown up with a dysfunctional background. His brothers had been teenagers when he was a baby and had grown into adults as pampered, indulged princes in a royal household, barely missing the mother forced to leave them behind with their father. None of their experiences had mirrored Raif's and their pity for him when they had later learned of the former Queen's alcoholism and fondness for young men had only lashed his pride, accentuated the differences between them and ensured that the brothers remained politely distant with each other.

'I have to make supper,' Claire told him.

Raif observed the standoffish cat and ignored it. He knew that, unlike dogs, cats didn't like to be courted. He took a seat and within a few minutes the cat made its approach. It paraded in front of him, showing off its sleek black elegance, big measuring green eyes locked to him. It folded into a relaxed repose at his feet. He let a careful fingertip drift down to stroke along its spine in a fleeting caress until it arched. A moment later, it had leapt onto his lap, the better to receive his admiration, and he smiled.

'Circe!' Claire called in reproof from the doorway.

'It's okay. I'm used to felines. My mother kept Siamese cats.' Interrupted, the cat sprang down from him and leapt back up onto the window seat.

'My mother took her in as a kitten and I

want to take her with me when I leave the island. It's a link, well, she's really the *only* link I have,' she admitted ruefully.

Raif rose lazily upright, every movement fluid, attracting her gaze. 'When did you lose your mother?'

'Last week. But it wasn't a surprise. She was terminally ill when I got here,' Claire explained in a troubled rush. 'Every day we had together was incredibly precious.'

'That's a very recent loss,' Raif murmured from the doorway as she returned to the vegetables she appeared to be chopping. He watched in some astonishment as she wielded a very sharp knife with the speed and efficiency of a professional.

'But just think, I mightn't have met her and got to know her at all,' Claire pointed out with a grimace at that concept. 'I was lucky. I'm so grateful I grabbed the chance to get to know her and didn't listen to everyone trying to stop me coming out here.'

'Who's everyone?'

'My boss, my stepmother, my boyfriend. Nobody wanted me to come here. But it was my one and only chance,' she admitted, big blue eyes wide. 'I had to take the chance... didn't I?'

'I agree. But what did it cost you?'

'The boyfriend and the job,' she confided wryly. 'But I would make the same choice again. It was worth it...*she* was worth it.'

Raif smiled slowly, his attention fully locked to the animation so vividly etched in her heart-shaped face. 'I'm glad of that for your sake. But how on earth did you forgive her for leaving you in the first place?'

Claire stiffened and paused to heap the diced vegetables into a bowl. 'If you had asked me that question a few years back, I would've said I *couldn't* forgive her,' she confided. 'But then my father passed away and my stepmother asked me to clear out my father's desk. She and my half-brother had to move, because it was a clergy house and it was needed for my father's replacement.'

'You didn't live with them?'

'No. I moved out as soon as I could afford a flat-share,' Claire admitted ruefully. 'My stepmother and I never jelled.'

Raif watched her move about the kitchen with surprising competence. She whipped out plates and reached for the bowl to carry them into the sitting room and lay the small table by the window. 'Take a seat,' she told him.

She trekked back into the kitchen and returned with a basket of bread, a bottle of water and two glasses. 'This is a very casual meal,' she warned him.

'You didn't have to feed me,' he told her gently.

'*I* was starving,' she replied.

'You mentioned clearing out your father's desk,' he reminded her. 'What did that have to do with anything?'

'I found all these letters my mother had sent over the years pleading for permission to see me,' Claire confided in a pained undertone. 'I was stunned. I was only told that she had met another man and run off with him. Nobody ever admitted that she had tried really hard to see me again. When my father agreed to the divorce, she let him have full custody because she felt guilty. She didn't appreciate that that meant that he could refuse to let her see me again and... she didn't have the money to take him to court.'

Raif helped himself to a portion of the

salad and some bread. 'Your father must've been very bitter.'

'Yes. He never forgave her for leaving him even though he remarried very soon after the divorce.' She leant forward, her face troubled. 'My mother, though, was only eighteen when she married him, and she gave birth to me within the year. Way too young to be married to a man fifteen years older and a mother,' she opined.

'Obviously she won your sympathy, but I feel some sympathy for your father,' Raif admitted. 'Fidelity in marriage is an expectation for most people. She was his wife and she betrayed his trust.'

Claire grimaced. 'She did. She went on holiday with her sister against his wishes and fell madly in love with a Greek fisherman. Eventually she married Kostas and they lived together in this house for almost fifteen years. He died at sea in a storm a few years ago and she stayed on here alone.'

Raif shrugged a broad shoulder and said gently, 'She was still an unfaithful wife.'

Claire sighed. 'Life isn't that black and white.'

'Sometimes it is,' Raif incised in disagreement. 'My father divorced my mother because he was bored. She did nothing wrong. She had given him three sons, and had been a good wife in every way, but he still ended their marriage. It destroyed her life. She lost almost everything that she valued and sank into depression.'

'That must have been really tough for her and you.' Claire looked thoughtful. 'What about your brothers?'

'They were almost grown at the time of the divorce and they remained with my father.'

'So, really you had no family support with the parent you were living with,' Claire registered in dismay on his behalf.

'This bread is incredibly good,' Raif remarked, reluctant to discuss his mother any further, some topics being too private. He had already shared much more than he usually did but now his reserve had kicked in.

Claire smiled. 'It should be. I trained as a pastry chef.'

Raif tucked into the seasonal salad with appreciation. He hadn't been that hungry but fresh, tasty food had a draw all of its own.

'Is your mother still alive?' she asked quietly.

'No, she's been gone for a few years now,' Raif confided. 'I can't imagine how you must feel meeting *your* mother after so long and discovering that you liked her...even though you weren't supposed to.'

'My father and stepmother raised me to be ashamed of her. They were very religious. That's why it was such a shock to read those letters. My father hung onto them even though he had no intention of letting us meet,' Claire said with distaste. 'I pictured him gloating over those letters, enjoying his power to deny her and me. That was his revenge. He was that kind of man.'

'You weren't close to him.'

'No, how could I have been? He could never see me as being a different person from my mother,' she pointed out ruefully. 'He had a son with my stepmother and he treated him very differently. He probably would have been happier had my mother taken me away with her. I was just the reminder of a marriage that had gone wrong and humiliated him.'

'I'm sorry you lost your mother so soon after finding her,' Raif murmured, pushing his empty plate away.

Claire's eyes prickled with moisture and she blinked rapidly. 'That's life,' she said with forced lightness of tone. 'What are you doing here on Kanos?'

As she began clearing the table, Raif stood up. 'I've been travelling for the last few weeks.'

'In a suit?'

'I had a business meeting this morning.'

Claire nodded slowly. 'It's been nice having company here for a change. The house feels so empty without my mother.'

'You have to give yourself time to grieve.'

'But I knew she was on borrowed time,' Claire protested chokily. 'I *should've* adjusted better.'

Watching a tear drip down her cheek, Raif closed a hand awkwardly to her shoulder and squeezed it. 'Preparing for a likelihood is not the same as dealing with the actual event.'

'Don't I know it?' she agreed wryly.

'I don't want to leave you here alone,' Raif admitted flatly.

Claire parted dry lips. 'Then *stay*... I'm not pushing you out.'

Raif sighed. 'You want company...and I want to kiss you.'

'Did I say kissing was off the table?' Claire reddened, fingernails biting into her palms as she voiced that uncharacteristically bold invitation while wondering what had come over her and why it seemed so important not to let him walk away.

'I won't take advantage of the fact that you feel lonely and sad,' Raif declared tautly. 'I'm not that kind of man.'

'But sometimes you have to go with the flow,' Claire muttered tautly.

Raif had never gone with the flow in his life. He worked to schedules based on a routine from which he rarely deviated, yet the concept of simply relaxing and following his own inclinations for even as long as an evening had immense appeal. 'Yes,' he conceded with a slow-burning smile of agreement.

'Nobody's waiting for you to return?' Claire prompted, her mouth drying at that possibility.

'Nobody.' A faint flush lined Raif's sculpted cheekbones, because the yacht had a crew of over sixty, not to mention his security team and admin staff. He knew very well what it was to be alone in a crowd of people, but he really didn't know what it was to be physically alone because from childhood there had always been domestic and security staff surrounding him.

Embarrassed by the tears she had let momentarily overpower her, Claire stacked the dishes busily and moved out to the kitchen with them.

Raif set the glasses uncertainly on the sink drainer. 'Leave them for now.'

'Tidy house, tidy mind,' Claire quipped. 'That was how I was brought up.'

'Does it make a difference?'

'No, it just keeps you constantly busy.'

Claire settled the dishes into the sink and began washing them and setting them on the drainer.

Raif hovered and then swept up the tea towel somewhat uneasily, vaguely recalling a woman drying dishes in one of the homes he had visited for the weekend while he was at boarding school.

'You don't have to help.'

'I can't stand here doing nothing.' Raif felt that he already spent far too much time doing nothing. He took care of Quristan's investments while running his development empire on the side. He had often been called a workaholic and saw no reason to disdain the label. He took pride in working to advance his country's interests and wealth. Or at least he had done so when he'd still believed that he could do a good job without infuriating his father. The recollection of his predicament made him bite back a groan. Well, he had never been a favoured son and now he never would be.

He reached for a plate and began to dry it with care, determined not to plunge himself into pointless self-recriminations. The Quristani government was pleased, the locals were ecstatic, and his father was outraged. There was nothing he could do about that. Many, many things in the modern world outraged King Jafri, who wished to remain a feudal ruler like his ancestors in a country with a democratically elected government. His father had been raised to be domineering, what he saw as 'strong'. But such methods only worked for an absolute monarch with unfettered power, such as his own father had been. And shorn of that

power, forced to accept government interference and advice, King Jafri had seethed
with frustration and the belief that he was
not being awarded the royal respect he saw
as his due.

Raif set down the plate, just as Claire
twitched the drying cloth from his fingers
and took over. He lounged back against the
fridge while she finished and stacked the
china back in a cabinet. As she passed by
him again, he propelled her gently back-
wards into his arms and pressed his mouth
to the slope of her shoulder, drinking in
the warm, lemony scent of her, and was almost lost to the steady pulse of arousal at
his groin. No woman had ever had such an
effect on him, but then he rarely allowed
himself to get close enough to be tempted.
Claire, however, had an indefinable quality that both relaxed and enticed him. She
was so honest, so natural, so much what he
needed in a woman to be attracted.

With a compulsive shiver, Claire leant
back into the heat and strength of him. She
had never been so intensely drawn to a guy
in her life and while in one sense it was
scary, in another it was wildly exciting. She

knew what she was inviting but she had no doubts. It was her decision if she chose to go to bed with someone, nobody else's. Her last boyfriend had tried to guilt her into sex and she had dug her heels in hard, needing more of a connection than she had found with him. It had never felt right with him. How was it that a stranger could connect with her so easily? How was it that she found Raif absolutely irresistible?

Squirming round in his light hold, Claire stretched up to find his mouth again and hunger ignited like a flame low in her tummy as his lips engulfed hers. It was what she had always sought and never found with a man: that crazy, uncontrollable surge of need to continue, to explore, to *experience*. It warmed the chill of loss inside her, gave her hope that her usual zest for life was within reach again.

Raif drew her back into the sitting room. 'Don't stop,' she told him, pausing the kiss only to refill her lungs.

'Where's your room?'

Claire laced her fingers into his and walked him into the first room off the sitting room, a freshly painted space her mother had had decorated for her in bright Mediterranean colours and fluttering, fringed arty drapes in advance of her arrival. It was the perfect backdrop for the unconventional, artistic daughter Jo had imagined Claire would be because Jo had liked to paint and make jewellery and pottery. Sadly, Claire was a girlie girl, who liked flowers and pastels, and she didn't think she had a single crafty, creative bone in her body. She liked to garden and she loved to cook, but she had never wanted to make stuff or wear anything bohemian that might make people raise a brow.

Sadness pulled at her and she pushed it away to the back of her mind. She wanted to celebrate life, seize it by the throat and go for it instead of following every careful cautious rule she had been raised with because that merely made her feel *scared*. Only in rebelling against those restrictions had she found her mother and begun to find out who she really was…

'I could do with a shower,' Raif confessed abruptly. 'I'm covered with salt from my swim.'

'I never thought of that,' Claire muttered,

showing him into the bathroom next door and pulling out a clean towel for his use.

She returned to her room and hovered. She wondered if she should tell him that he would be her first while also wondering whether he was deliberately giving her a chance to change her mind. No, why would he do that? Men didn't do that when a woman seemed confident, did they? Determined to commit to her decision, she stripped and dropped her clothing in the laundry hamper before scrambling into the bed. For the very first time, she felt she was with the right man. There was a connection, an understanding she couldn't explain but it was a great deal more than she had ever felt before.

Raif stood under the slow flow of lukewarm water in a daze. He was nervous. He knew that he wasn't supposed to be, but he was. He was about to ditch a lifetime of celibacy and he was about to do it in the heat of a reckless moment. But Claire made him *feel* reckless, and that was an indulgence he had never tasted before, and he wanted more of that feeling. She gave him a sense of pure freedom and joy, a feeling that was equally rare in his world. She wanted him and he wanted her. It was straightforward and simple. There was no need to make it into something more challenging or meaningful than it was. Once he had thought that he would save the experience for his bride and now he questioned that he had ever been that naïve.

Raif strode into the bedroom, the damp towel wrapped round his waist. 'Still think I'm beautiful?' he teased.

Just looking at him, Claire ran out of breath all at once. He was like a lean, mean fighting machine out of an action movie, his abdomen laced and indented with hard muscle, biceps flexing below smooth brown skin as he tossed the towel aside. 'Yes,' she said without hesitation.

Laughing, Raif swung into the bed beside her and closed her into his arms. His mouth caressed hers and his tongue pried between her lips, darting and delving and sending a rush of splintering energy through her. Hunger was a hot pool of liquidity at the centre of her, a pulse point of growing desire. Her hips squirmed into the mattress as his hands came up to cup her full breasts, thumbs brushing her swollen nipples.

'You're the beautiful one,' he murmured, pressing her back into the pillows, staring appreciatively down at her as her honey-blonde hair tumbled across the dark linen, her cornflower-blue eyes wide with disconcertion against her flushed cheeks, her lips swollen from his kisses. He drank in the warmth in that scrutiny like a starving man.

He lowered his mouth to a rosy peak and sucked strongly, every fantasy fulfilled because she was the most glorious mix of soft and firm, silky and luscious. Her hands ran up over his corrugated abdomen to his shoulders in exploration and he shifted with sensual pleasure thrumming through him like an intoxicating drug, his spine bowing as she trailed her hands down over his back.

His skin was smooth, and he was so warm that she revelled in every path she took across his body, so different from her own and yet equally responsive. Every tug of his lips on her nipple sent an arrow of electric heat straight down into her pelvis. His hands roamed deftly over her curves and then he pulled her back into his arms to

ravish her mouth again with a wild intensity
that thrilled her. He was exploring now, trac-
ing her inner thighs, locating the most tender
spot of all and circling there gently before
dipping a finger between her slick folds.

'Oh...' she moaned, the hollow ache between her thighs now joined by an inner
clenching sensation as excitement and anticipation built.

'Are you on contraception?' he asked her
without warning.

'No...' Claire stilled to stare up at him.
All of a sudden, he sounded very serious
and yet anxious too.

Raif groaned and began to pull back from
her. 'I don't have a condom. We should've
talked about this sooner.'

Claire's brow had furrowed. 'You don't
carry anything?' she said in surprise.

'I don't have any reason to...well, I didn't
until now.'

Claire sat up, her cheeks burning. 'Well,
I have a condom.'

'That's a relief.' Raif watched as she
scrambled out of bed and dug into the bat-
tered wardrobe to extract a handbag from
which she took a small foil packet. 'My

mother insisted I carried one round…just in case,' she explained uncomfortably. 'She thought I was weird because I'm still a virgin and she didn't want me to—'

Raif froze in shock. 'You're a virgin?'

Claire wrinkled her nose in embarrassment. 'You think it's weird too, don't you? But in the household I grew up in, where premarital sex was a hanging offence, I didn't dare experiment. I couldn't face being accused of being promiscuous like my mother. I was too scared of my father…and then as I got older, it got harder to cross that bridge. Gosh, I'm gabbling!'

'You don't need to be embarrassed.' Raif caught the tiny packet she tossed at him and sat up to reach for her hand and pull her back to him. 'I'm not very experienced either… for reasons I prefer not to go into right now.'

It was Claire's turn to still, gazing up into those stunning golden caramel eyes of his, accentuated by spiky black lashes. He was gorgeous. How could he possibly be inexperienced?

'So, you'll have to make allowances for me,' Raif told her gruffly.

Claire smiled. 'As long as you do the same for me,' she whispered shyly.

He curved her back into his arms, tumbling her back into the pillows with renewed confidence. 'I don't need to make allowances. All I need to do is fully appreciate you,' he declared with a roughened sound low in his throat as he ran his big hands over her.

He kissed her and her heart started beating insanely fast. Her hands crept up the back of his neck to tangle in his luxuriant silky hair and smooth over his skull. A curl of heat snaked through her, swiftly followed by another, the same hunger tugging at her again. He traced the hot liquid centre of her again and it was almost unbearable, her body ramping up tension and need faster than she could control it. She squirmed, a gasp parting her lips, wanting more, not even quite knowing what more was but knowing that the way she felt she wanted it yesterday.

'I know,' he groaned, running his mouth down the valley between her breasts. 'But you're not ready yet.'

'I feel ready,' Claire said unevenly.

'I don't want to hurt you,' Raif muttered

thickly, sliding down her restless body, pressing his mouth gently to her writhing length, pausing and lingering at the most sensitive place of all.

Shocked by that sensual assault though she was, she was instantly plunged into a world of intense sensation. Halfway through demanding that he stop, she realised that if he stopped she would probably kill him because exquisite sensation had destroyed all resistance. Now she was twisting and jerking and moaning, the hollow ache between her thighs merely strengthening in intensity. And then the tension pushing up through her tightened every muscle in her body and the surge of her climax blew her away. She literally saw stars, cried out as the sweet convulsions of pleasure engulfed her and the aftermath of peace flooded her.

'Now you're ready,' Raif told her raggedly.

And she couldn't have spoken at that moment to save her life. He tipped her back and slid into her, slow and sure; her body seemed to accept the fullness of him. She stayed very still, wildly conscious of his every movement, tilting back her knees, feeling the push of his lean strong hips as he gathered power and sank deeper into her resisting flesh. And resist her body did.

He paused, melting dark eyes holding hers levelly. 'I'm worried about hurting you.'

'I always expected it to hurt the first time,' Claire confided fatalistically.

Raif was incredibly tense.

'Don't stop,' she urged.

And that galvanised him into action. He drew back and surged into her once more and a sharp, tearing pain made her cry out.

'I guess this isn't quite a fantasy experience for you,' Claire quipped, gathering her breath again, hoping he hadn't noticed the inadvertent tears that had filled her eyes. Raising her hips to his and angling back, she locked her legs round him in encouragement.

With a ragged groan, he succumbed, pushing deeper. 'You feel so good,' he bit out rawly. 'Like hot liquid silk enclosing me.'

The friction of his invasion made every nerve ending sit up and take notice. His rhythm vanquished her discomfiture, persuaded her to move in concert, no longer a bystander but a full participant. The wave of excitement gripped her afresh as his pace quickened and then he was groaning over her, her body jerking from the fierce onslaught of his orgasm.

'It'll be easier the next time,' she told him soothingly as he gazed down at her in a fierce combination of satisfaction, guilt and apology.

'There'll be a next time?' he muttered in a daze. 'A second chance?'

The most extraordinary wave of tenderness flooded her. She had never felt as close to another person as she felt to him at that moment. 'If you want one,' she whispered, wrapping her arms round him, smoothing the tension from his broad shoulders, watching the stress ebb from him again.

'I want one,' he confessed with a brilliant smile that filled her with warmth. 'I want you.'

'But we don't have any protection, so you'll have to pull out…or something,' she warned in a rush.

Raif continued to hold her close, stroking her hair back from her flushed face, revelling in her generosity and warmth. 'It was special,' he murmured softly. 'Very special because it was with you.'

With reluctance, he eased back from her and his ebony brows flared up in consternation as he muttered something in his own language. 'The condom split...'

'Oh, dear...' Claire could think of nothing else to say while she wondered how long that little foil packet had been lying around before her mother embarrassed her by forcing it on her.

His lean darkly handsome face shadowed. 'I was rough with you. That's probably why.'

'You weren't rough,' she scolded quietly. 'Don't say that.'

'Why do I feel like I've known you for ever?' Raif studied her with a frown of bewilderment before he left to go into the bathroom and clean up.

'Are you leaving?' Claire called in his wake.

'Are you joking? After you offered me a second chance?' Raif teased.

And Claire laughed and relaxed, relieved that he was staying and that any awkwardness had dissipated. He returned to the bed, switched off the light and gathered her into his arms as if he had been doing it all his life.

Claire woke up with a start and found herself alone. Naked, she got out of bed, yanked her wrap off the back of the door and went to check the rest of the house. Raif had gone. But on the table by the window there was a note printed with a phone number.

'In case of consequences or if you simply want to keep in touch.'

But he was *gone*, and a terrible hollowness spread through Claire. What had she expected? A one-night stand with a stranger would rarely lead to the start of anything more lasting. It was done and dusted and she would never see him again.

Her heart ached as if it had been squeezed dry. It hurt. At the time she had told herself that parting wouldn't hurt but she had lied to herself because she wasn't that tough, wasn't that unfeeling. In an incredibly short space of time, Raif had come to mean something to her. He had been kind, caring, warm, affectionate, everything she craved in a man and had never found, but how hard was it to be any of those things when he was only planning to be around for a few hours?

And now it was back to real life. Work at twelve down in the harbour bar where she cooked and waitressed at weekends, the only employment currently available to her and with tips and pay just enough to cover the rent. Yannis, who owned the bar, was hoping to give her more work over the summer when the marina got busier and tourists arrived. But there was no dependable flow of trade on an island as small as Kanos. Sometimes the boats called in, sometimes, they didn't bother. That was why she needed to return to the UK. There was no reliable winter employment for someone like her.

She stepped into the shower. How weak was it that she wanted to make use of that phone number already? How sad was that? As she got dressed, she could not help reliving the night that had passed. The second time had been amazing. He had taught her what pleasure was all about, but they had discovered it together, which had somehow made it more intense and meaningful, only how meaningful could it be when they had been a couple for just a single night? And he had left in the early hours before she even awakened? Why was she being sad and immature? Why wasn't she accepting the reality of what had happened between them? A flashfire attraction that flared and passed? He had said he was travelling. Of course, she wasn't likely to see him again. At least he hadn't made her any empty promises.

Dressed in frayed denim shorts and a tee shirt, she opened the door to head out for work and froze. A giant basket of roses adorned with glittery balloons sat outside. She laughed out loud and reached for the card envelope. The card simply read, 'Raif'. No words. After all, what was there to say? But a huge smile had wiped away her frown as she rushed indoors and began to drag out vases and carefully settle her beautiful flowers in water. What a wonderful, thoughtful gesture! He hadn't stayed until she wakened and maybe that had been for the best, she conceded reluctantly. What had there been left to say but goodbye?

CHAPTER THREE

RAIF STOOD ON the sun deck staring out to sea.

He had done what he had to do, so why did he feel so bad about it? Claire was wonderful but there could be no future for them. There was nowhere for a relationship to go. He was in love with another woman and had been for years. He couldn't offer Claire the whole heart that she deserved. He didn't want some sleazy occasional affair, did he?

Even so, he had never wanted any woman the way he wanted her and that acknowledgement shook him. He had never thought of Nahla that way. She was another man's wife, the mother of children. Hell...she was his third cousin's wife! He had always appreciated the barriers between them and remained respectful in thought and deed. Claire, however, had the most amazing lu-

minous sex appeal, he conceded abstract-
edly, registering that he had barely recalled
his father's fury since he first saw Claire on
that beach.

Yannis, the bar owner was already rearrang-
ing chairs round a large table outside when
Claire walked into the village. 'We've got a
big party coming in around eight from one
of the yachts,' he warned her. 'I asked Sofia
to come in and serve to leave you free in the
kitchen.'

'How big is "big"?' Claire asked.

'Ten, no children. Someone's birthday
bash,' he told her cheerfully. 'They're bring-
ing their own cake.'

'Well, that will save some time.' Claire
laughed because the place was empty aside
of a couple of elderly regulars propping up
the bar. She would have had plenty of time
to knock up a cake, had she so desired.

'I told Sofia to tell her sister to bring us
in a load of fresh veg,' Yannis told her with
pride. 'You see, I do think ahead.'

'You do,' Claire conceded, walking out
back to the kitchen to check on the other

supplies, which the older man often over-
looked when unexpected customers arrived.

She had studied for three years to become
a pastry chef and copious working experience had been included in her degree course.
In fact, only the year before she had got a
position as a pastry chef at a top restaurant.
Unhappily, that was the job she had had to
give up when she'd decided to fly out to
Greece to be with her mother. Claire, however, was pragmatic about that sacrifice.
Chefs were always in demand, and when
she got back to the UK she would soon find
a job, even if it didn't have quite the presti-
gious status of the one she had quit. Eventually she would climb back up the ladder
and start paying off her student loans again.

Her father had thoroughly disapproved
of her chosen career. In truth the only version of her future that would have pleased
her father would have been her marrying
some approved man in his congregation and
settling down to raise children. Her half-
brother, Tom, had just entered theological
college and, last she had heard, already had
a church placement waiting for him. Claire
was willing to admit that the long and often

late hours in the catering trade were a drawback but, aside of that, she enjoyed cooking and loved the frantically busy pace of a working kitchen.

She spent the afternoon baking bread and a selection of desserts and pastries. It was a busy evening. Yannis dropped in to tell her that her food, the desserts in particular, had received many compliments. Around finishing time, she was invited out to meet the customers. 'I think I may have found you a cheap way of getting home,' Yannis told her.

A personable middle-aged man introduced himself as Captain Hastings of the *Mahnoor*. Her brows rose when she realised that he was referring to the giant yacht that resembled a cruise liner anchored out in the bay.

'Are you interested in temporary employment?' he asked. 'We'll be docking in Southampton in just over two months. Our assistant chef broke a leg mountaineering and he's out of commission. We need a replacement for the rest of the trip.'

'I'm Gregoire, the head chef,' a bald older man with a thick French accent interposed. 'Tell me about your training and experience.'

Someone pulled up a chair for her and there was a flurry of introductions to the crew seated round the table. About a quarter were women.

Gregoire asked exacting questions but hope and anticipation were already bubbling up inside Claire. Working onboard a yacht sailing back to the UK would solve all her problems. She wouldn't have travel expenses and she would be able to save her salary, which would give her a cushion of cash towards affording accommodation on arrival.

'I think you'll do, and you'll pick up useful experience on the yacht,' Gregoire pronounced.

Claire breathed in deep. 'Can I bring my cat? She's well trained.'

The captain frowned and rubbed his chin. 'I don't see why not as long as you keep her under control.'

'She hasn't got pet travel papers yet.'

'You can get that taken care of at one of our ports of call.'

The yacht was moving on the next morning and naturally that was when they wanted her to start. It didn't suit. She would have liked longer to pack up, but she knew that

Sofia would happily donate her mother's possessions to the local charity she supported and she herself would only be a retaining a few small keepsakes because nothing else made sense in her situation. After staying for a drink with the younger crew members and getting to know Liz, the onboard beauty consultant, and a couple of cabin stewards, Claire began to look forward to her new job.

'Oh, I forgot to ask. Who owns the yacht or is it on a private charter?' she asked.

'His Royal Highness, the Prince—'

'Royalty?' She gasped.

'Foreign royalty. So rich I'm surprised he doesn't shed diamonds or drip oil as he walks. You don't need to worry though. You almost never see him. He works on board. He's some gobsmackingly important big business whizz. He has a large party of guests joining us, though, so we'll all be run off our feet this trip,' she forecast.

Raif wakened at dawn and headed straight into the gym as was his wont. An elegant black cat awaited him there, a cat called Circe, which belonged to someone on the crew. Raif had tried to ignore the cat because it plunged him into memories he preferred not to recall. But the cat was persistent and refused to be ignored, following him back to his private quarters and graciously allowing him a brief caress before he stepped into the shower.

How many black cats like Circe lived around the Mediterranean ports? Probably thousands, he reasoned, and at least fifty with the name of a Greek goddess. In any case, he had only noticed the cat since they had docked in Trieste, where presumably the new crew member had boarded. Since then, the sleek black cat had become a ship mascot. As far as he knew he was the cat's first port of call on its wanderings. It visited the captain on the bridge every morning and, apparently, the unsentimental older man had shopped for fresh fish for the cat's benefit and Raif's famous head chef had created some special dish for it.

The cat visited the entire crew at different times of day. It had its own bed in the beauty parlour and toys in the office of Raif's admin staff. In the afternoon, it slumbered in Raif's office. So self-possessed and fearless was the cat that Raif would not have been surprised to find it kicking back on a sun lounger with a fat cigar and a tumbler of the most expensive whisky on board. It took adoration as its due.

But worst of all, it reminded Raif of Claire and he didn't need the reminders when he was peculiarly conscious of every mile that took him further from her. She had texted him once to thank him for the flowers but had not contacted him again. Why would she have when he had neither responded to that text nor contacted her? No doubt he would have heard from her had she been pregnant but, since he had not heard from her, he told himself that he should be grateful that that unforgettable night had not ended in a conception. Only, at heart, he knew he wasn't grateful when he still couldn't get either Claire or that extraordinary night out of his head.

Several decks below the owner's suite, Claire was contemplating the pregnancy test she had finally purchased at their last port. It had taken her two missed periods to accept that there could be genuine cause for alarm. The first month she had assumed it was stress from losing her mother, but the second month panic had begun to build inside her. It truly hadn't occurred to her that she might fall pregnant the very first time she had sex or that the repercussions from one night with a guy could be that massive. As she groaned out loud at her stupidity, her foolish naïve confidence in her sound judgement, she looked around her comfortable cabin for the comfort of her pet...her *roving* pet. Of course, as usual, Circe was absent.

Penning up Circe for a large part of the day hadn't worked and eventually the cat had slid out of a porthole and discovered that there was very large and interesting boat filled with people to explore. There had been no caging Circe after that and as Claire's pet had ranged far and wide and she'd realised that the cat wasn't annoying anyone, she had relaxed and stopped worrying. Now she only locked up Circe when she went ashore and that had been only a handful of times because there was no room in her budget for shopping trips when she had to save up.

In truth, she acknowledged, she loved working on the yacht. The pay was terrific and the accommodation top of the line. There were enough other women onboard to ensure she had company when she wanted it and there were all sorts of extras on the *Mahnoor*. When there were no guests, they were allowed to use the beauty salon where Liz, the resident beauty consultant and massage therapist, was going mad with boredom. They also had access to a pool and a gym and the latest movies.

But she still worked long hours and, although she had enjoyed the sheer frantic pace of the galley while catering to a large demanding party of well-heeled guests, she was glad that the last event of their stay was due that morning, a barbecue on the top deck. It would be the first time she had been allowed near the upper decks to which only senior crew members enjoyed access. Once the guests disembarked, there would be perfect peace and nothing taxing for the remainder of her trip back to London.

She did the test for which she had prepared and sat down again to await the result. Would Raif help as he had implied in his note? She had been tempted so often to phone or text him, but he had pretty much ghosted her, had certainly not started up a conversation when she'd thanked him for the flowers. Where did he even live? She knew nothing about him. Would he offer her financial help? Or had he just offered support without ever meaning to do anything concrete?

Claire peered at the result and felt sick, indeed as nauseous as she had felt on several occasions in recent days. She had sore breasts and couldn't stand the taste of coffee any longer. The nausea came and went at different times of the day but the extreme tiredness and the sleeping like the dead at night was there all the time. It was positive, pretty much what she had expected, and shock and fright vibrated through her and she had to dash into the bathroom to lose her early lunch in the most undignified way possible.

The extravagant furnishings on the busy top deck blew Claire away as she assembled plates at the built-in barbecue service counter for the lunch. Wonderfully attractive, shapely women strolled around in minimal bikinis. One in particular caught her eye because she was a famous supermodel and so gorgeous that she looked as unreal as a beautiful doll. Long black hair like silk streamed down her narrow spine, a big hat sheltering her perfect photogenic face from the sun's rays. Her beautiful body was close to naked in a thong bikini that revealed her bottom and all of her long, long legs, her feet clad in very high heels. A special carpet had been put down to protect the floor of the deck.

Glancing away from the beauty, Claire was craning her neck to catch a glimpse of the prince. As the crowd round the top table moved, she saw a middle-aged man with a trio of what might have been bodyguards stationed behind him. That had to be him, she thought, although she didn't know why the other females on board had insisted that she was in for a treat when she saw His Royal Highness.

A sudden shriek erupted from the gorgeous brunette and Claire turned back in disbelief to see something black hit the hard wall with a crunch and fall. It was Circe. She looked on, refusing to believe what she was seeing.

At her elbow, Gregoire said something unrepeatable in French.

The brunette was having hysterics. 'It touched my leg. Everybody knows I can't stand animals anywhere near me!' she screeched accusingly.

'You didn't need to kick it and hurt it!' someone else commented.

Claire crept out from behind the counter to approach her cat's still body. Gregoire reappeared at her elbow with a large serving salver. Before Claire did anything, he eased his hands very gently below Circe and lifted the animal onto it. 'We'll get a vet,' he told her. 'We'll get a vet immediately.'

'See that is done directly,' another voice continued, a very familiar English drawl, unusually clipped and curt and unmistakeably commanding.

Claire glanced up, her eyes rounding with pure incredulity. Raif was standing over both of them. He angled his head at one of the other men standing nearby and he hurried off. 'Raif...?' she whispered weakly.

'Please continue serving,' he urged Gregoire as he held out his hands to take charge of Circe. 'Let my guests enjoy their last party.'

After a disconcerted pause, the chef passed the injured animal over to Raif.

'I will ensure that the cat receives the very best attention,' he declared.

'Not without me,' Claire chipped in helplessly, taken aback by his sudden appearance. 'Are you one of the guests?'

And Raif looked at her properly for the first time and froze in consternation, his tortoiseshell eyes widening before he dipped his black lashes to conceal his reaction. It occurred to her then that he hadn't recognised her, not with a chef's cap and net hiding her hair, not in her shapeless kitchen scrubs. 'I'm so sorry about this. I shouldn't have brought her onboard,' she muttered. 'I can't bear to see her hurt.'

'Claire, we will go inside and allow you to recover from the shock of this…incident.' Raif selected the word with care and rested a light hand at her spine to direct her towards the nearest door. She preceded him into a very spacious living area decorated with the utmost luxury and elegance.

One of the bodyguards she had seen in the

crew canteen appeared and addressed Raif in another language.

'A car is already waiting at the quay to take you to the vet. The cat will have to be scanned for injuries and we can't offer that facility onboard. Mohsin will accompany you.'

Claire watched Mohsin bow low and her mouth ran dry. An awful, impossible suspicion was occurring to her. It should have been impossible. Raif could not be *the* royal prince, who owned the vast yacht, could he? 'Let *my* guests enjoy their last party,' he had said, indicating that he was the host and, truly, he had taken charge to the manner born, hurrying her indoors to ensure that she said and did nothing that could offend.

She was shaken and horrified and furious all at one and the same time. He had pretended to be someone ordinary...*hadn't he*? He had concealed his identity, misled her. Understanding and realisation set in hard. Dear heaven, she was working for him and he hadn't known...hadn't known she was on his wretched yacht until he'd recognised her! Whichever way she looked at the situation, it was an embarrassing mess for both of them and when she added in the reality that he had got her pregnant, the mess turned into a complete disaster!

The bodyguard removed the salver holding Circe from her frozen hands and angled his chin at another door. 'You come this way?' he said in guttural English.

Raif was staring at her, full-on staring as if he had never seen a woman before. Claire turned scarlet, suddenly aware of how unflattering her working garb was and hurriedly turning away to follow the older man holding open a door on the other side of the room for her.

Raif watched her depart. She was so small. How had he forgotten how small she was? He could not credit that she was working on the yacht. Circe was hers but naturally it had not crossed his mind that Claire could be on the *Mahnoor*. She had said she was a chef, and he had seen her at the counter, but until she'd looked up at him with those very blue eyes, he had not recognised her.

How long had she been on board? All these weeks when he had been thinking about her, wondering about her, she had been within reach and only a few decks below him. He did not participate in the hiring of crew members because that was the captain's job. How could he have guessed that she was no longer on the island? Had he phoned her as he had been tempted to do, he would have found out, he conceded ruefully. But then what could he have done with the knowledge that she was on his yacht? He did not and would not harass anyone who worked for him and anything of a personal nature would be inappropriate and indiscreet.

Claire followed the bodyguard down a long companionway and then downstairs to a gangway and on to the quay where a long white gleaming limousine awaited them. He set the salver carefully into the back seat and stood until she had slid in beside her immobile pet and then he climbed into the front passenger seat beside the driver.

She stroked a fingertip along the cat's spine. Her eyes were wet and scratchy with unshed tears. She wouldn't be able to bear it if Circe died. Had she noticed the cat mingling with the guests she would have removed her. After all, she understood that not everyone liked animals…but had that awful woman had to kick Circe with such violence? Circe must have brushed against her legs, had possibly given the beauty a fright. The nausea in Claire's tummy increased. It was shock, shock at everything that had happened.

In her mind's eye, she saw Raif poised in the saloon again, sheathed in a lightweight summer suit that only a man as formal as he was would have worn to such an event. But linking that version of Raif to the Raif she had met and liked and laughed with two months earlier was impossible for her. His reaction to the attack on Circe had been so polished, so smooth, so reserved.

Mohsin ushered her into a smart surgery where they were immediately attended by a veterinary nurse, who, clearly expecting their arrival, took charge of Circe and bore her off. Claire sat down shakily in the waiting area, trying not to wonder what such attention and treatment would cost, and all the time she was blaming herself for not restricting her cat's freedom once the guests came onboard. She had been thoughtless, *stupid* and in the same way she had been reckless and stupid with Raif. It was a bitter truth that continuing to follow her father's rigid rules of behaviour would have kept her safe. Asserting her independence and taking advantage of her freedom to do as she liked had steered her down a dangerous path. What could she possibly offer her baby as a single parent without even a decent income?

Mohsin approached her with a cardboard cup of cold water. 'The Prince will make everything all right again,' he assured her confidently.

No, he wouldn't. The Prince would be severely challenged to make anything right in her life again, although it was perfectly possible that he would hope that she was willing to terminate her pregnancy. But she wasn't prepared to even consider that option. She pulled off her hairnet, cap and apron and folded them together neatly.

The door opened and she glanced up. More than an hour had passed since their arrival. She tensed when she saw Raif speaking to the receptionist. He addressed her in fluent French and a few moments later, an older man appeared and began to speak to

Raif at length. That conversation concluded, Raif approached her.

'What's happening?' she whispered apprehensively.

'Circe requires careful surgery but that will not take place until later when the requisite surgeon arrives. Her leg is fractured and she has concussion. It is safest for her to remain here under supervision for the present,' he advised.

Claire nodded very slowly. 'Is she likely to survive this?'

'Assuming there are no further complications with the head injury.'

Claire swallowed thickly.

'We will leave now,' Raif decreed.

She wanted to ask if she could see Circe again, but didn't want to make demands, and all the time she was frantically worrying about what all this veterinary attention and treatment would cost. Surgery here in Monte Carlo for an animal would not be cheap. 'I don't know how I'm going to pay for this,' she mumbled shakily.

Raif reached for her hand. 'That is not a concern you need consider. *My* guest caused the injuries at my party. I cannot abide cruelty to animals,' he bit out in a curt undertone. 'I am responsible for ensuring that this situation is put right…as far as it can be.'

Claire tugged her chilled fingers free and whispered, 'I can't let you pay the bill. It wouldn't be right.'

Raif sighed as he accompanied her outside where it seemed a whole fleet of vehicles awaited them. There were men standing about with earpieces, his security guards. She wondered absently where they had been hidden while he'd spent half the night with her. Bitter resentment and anger bubbled up through her again.

She was shown into another limousine and he slid in beside her, prompting her to move to the far end of the seat. Her hands twisted the folded kitchen apparel on her lap as the silence thickened.

'Claire.'

Her head whipped round, blue eyes bright as sapphires with temper. 'I'm not speaking to you. I don't know you. I want nothing to do with you. I will do the job I was hired to do and hopefully our paths won't cross again. Thankfully, we'll be back in the UK in ten days.'

Even as she spoke, she was wondering how she could possibly adhere to her statement. She was pregnant with his child. She had to tell him, didn't she? It wouldn't be fair not to tell him, would it? It would be wrong to remain silent and her unborn baby deserved more consideration from her. Her teeth gritted.

Raif said nothing. She was entitled to her feelings even if they conflicted with his own. Unfortunately, life was not quite so simple and straightforward as she would like it to be, and he owed her an explanation for his behaviour.

CHAPTER FOUR

'WHERE ARE WE?' Claire demanded abruptly as the limousine drove down a lane with a high concealing hedge and drew up outside a large white villa. She immediately blamed herself for getting so lost in her own thoughts that she had not even noticed where they were going. Of course, she hadn't known they were travelling to anywhere other than back to the busy harbour and the yacht, so she had not paid attention.

'This is my home in Monte Carlo. I want to speak to you, and it would be indiscreet to seek a private interview with you on the *Mahnoor*,' he pointed out. 'Here we may talk in private without fear of awakening speculation.'

'So, you're kidnapping me to protect my reputation and yours,' Claire deduced.

'Don't be ridiculous. Clearly, you are angry with me.'

'Gosh, you can really read the room, can't you?' she mocked with a toss of her head.

Raif forestalled further argument by getting out of the car. She thought about sitting on in the car alone like a truculent schoolgirl. Her cheeks reddened and as the door beside her opened, she climbed straight out.

'Tea or coffee?' Raif enquired politely as an older woman greeted him in the hall.

'Tea…and a cloakroom?' Claire asked stiltedly.

At the vanity unit of the very fancy cloakroom, she splashed her face, washed her hands and finger-combed her tousled hair. She leant on the sink and said a prayer for her pet's well-being. The tears threatened to overflow again. She didn't know what was wrong with her because she had never been someone who cried easily and yet recently the most foolish things could make her eyes water. It could be her surging hormones. She recalled her friend, Lottie's tears while she was pregnant. Lottie had sworn that pregnancy had turned her into a watering pot. Claire sighed heavily and turned

away from the unflattering mirror, knowing
that she looked pale and drawn because she
didn't bother with make-up when she was
in the galley preparing food as the heat only
melted it off again and left her face streaky.

She walked back out to the hall and espied Raif standing in a plush drawing room
furnished in opulent shades of cream and
sage green. It looked as new as though nobody had ever set foot in it, sat on one of
the sofas or so much as dared to crease a
single cushion.

The older woman appeared with a tray
and set it down on the coffee table. Claire
looked at Raif and then wished she hadn't
because for a split second before he saw her,
his expression was unguarded and his tension, his discomfiture showed. As the refreshments arrived, he unfroze and smiled at
the woman, thanking her. It was his habit to
make an effort to fit into any situation, she
conceded heavily, remembering him inex-
pertly trying to wield a drying cloth at the
cottage, trying to be as ordinary as he was
not ordinary.

And yet the perfectly tailored lines of his
casual light blue suit, trousers taut against

his long muscular thighs, his jacket merely accentuating his wide, hard torso, narrow waist and broad shoulders, spoke of his high income. There was nothing ordinary about a guy so gorgeous that she had a compulsive need to stare at him. His lean features were flawless. Why hadn't she smelt a rat in the sudden appearance of such masculine perfection on a public beach? There he had stood stripping in the bay, burnished male beauty and strength in every honed line of him. Nothing ordinary about that or those amazing dark golden eyes below his ridiculously long, lush black lashes. She should have been suspicious and cautious, and she had been neither.

Aware her breathing had shortened and her body heated while she scrutinised him, Claire looked away fast, but he was still freshly imprinted back in her brain. Even now, she stuck by her original belief that he was the epitome of male beauty and it had blinded her.

'You should have told me that you were a blasted prince!' Claire condemned as she leant forward, desperate to occupy her restless hands, and poured the tea into the china cups.

'What difference would it have made?'

'Well, for a start if I'd known that yacht was yours, I'd never have taken a job on it!' she fired back unanswerably.

Raif compressed his lips. 'There is little point in exchanging what ifs or might-have-beens. You cannot blame me for an accident of birth.'

'You're a *royal*, for goodness' sake!' she reminded him sharply.

'A minor one. I'm third in the line of succession after my father but I have two older brothers, both married and likely to produce male heirs and the birth of each child will push me further down the inheritance line,' he explained. 'I grew up in the UK. I'm not an important person in Quristan.'

'And you're very rich,' Claire remarked. 'I would never have got involved with you had I known how unequal we were in status.'

'Attraction trumps all such differences. At the time such thoughts weren't important to either of us. I did not set out to mislead you in any way,' he countered gently.

'But you were happy to *avoid* telling me about your real status.'

'Was that so wrong? To enjoy being accepted simply as a man? I had had an altercation with my father that morning. I found freedom and peace in that cove for a few minutes of relaxation.'

'And then I entered the picture and everything went to hell,' Claire inserted doggedly.

'I have not a single regret about what happened between us,' Raif told her with conviction. 'It was the most real connection I have ever enjoyed with a woman. Why would I wish that we had never met at all?'

'You'll regret it deeply once I tell you what I have to tell you,' Claire warned him tautly.

Raif frowned as he lifted his tea from the tray. 'So, talk…'

'I've done a test and I'm pregnant,' Claire informed him quietly.

He set down the tea with a jarring rattle of china. 'Are you sure of this?'

'The test was positive.'

He was pale now, his bone structure starkly outlined by his tension. 'I didn't think—'

'No, neither did I,' Claire cut in. 'But we took a lot of risks that night. We had the accident with the contraception and then we went ahead twice more without protection.'

His high cheekbones were edged with slight colour now. He had taken to sex with all the enthusiasm of a sex-starved healthy man. He had run an insane risk with very little encouragement. Keeping his hands off Claire had proved impossible and the withdrawal method he had sought to embrace had been more challenging than he had envisaged. He had had no restraint, no control with her and that was one very good reason why he had left her before he could succumb to the temptation of waking her up *again*. And still he wakened every morning, remembering the hot, tight glory of her curvaceous body writhing against his own and the high of every single climax they had shared. She had blown his every expectation out of the water and he had gloried in every indulgent moment of their intimacy.

And now she was carrying his child. That knowledge stunned Raif. He could barely credit it when he had assumed that he would never have a family of his own. 'When did you find out?'

'Today. I didn't do the test until I had to.

I was avoiding it, burying my head in the sand. I'm at least two months along already,' she admitted uncomfortably.

He pulled out his phone and rang a number, spoke in French to whoever was answering and at length. 'We will see a doctor together this evening if it can be arranged. We need official confirmation of that test of yours before we go any further.'

'There isn't a possibility of a mistake,' she protested. 'And I need to get back to work. The excuse of needing a few hours off to take care of Circe has lasted long enough.'

'You can't work in a kitchen when you're pregnant,' Raif said with a straight face that told her he was being completely serious in voicing that belief. 'You could have an accident. You could hurt yourself or the baby.'

'Raif,' Claire murmured gently. 'Pregnant women have been cooking on everything from campfires to stoves for thousands of years.'

His ebony brows drew together. '*You* will not. I do not want anything to happen to either of you. I am sure any doctor would agree with me.'

'So, you're presumably not hoping that I

will consider a termination or an adoption?'
Claire gathered with relief at that reasonable
assumption.

'Of course not. A child is precious and I
could not bear to part with my own flesh
and blood,' he responded, frowning again.
'How could you think that I would want or
dare to suggest such remedies?'

'We don't know each other well enough
for me to assume how you are likely to respond to this situation. But I do assure you
that no doctor is likely to tell you that it's
dangerous for me to cook,' Claire stated
wryly.

His phone buzzed and he answered it with
a frown, which slowly cleared. A couple of
minutes later, he shoved the phone back into
his pocket. 'We have an appointment with
an obstetrician in an hour,' he informed her.

Money talks, she thought in wry acceptance, grateful that she hadn't blurted that
provocative belief out loud. But Circe had
received instant access to treatment and now
Claire would not have to await a medical appointment in the normal way. That was the
privileged world that Raif lived in, a world
that operated, it seemed, on the power of

wealth and influence. But his attitude was not what she had expected in any way. She had thought he might be angry, even denying any knowledge of her or implying that perhaps the child could not be his. She had been prepared for the worst reactions and the unkindest suggestions, yet she had been absolutely wrong. The discovery shook her.

'We will have a late lunch now,' Raif continued smoothly.

'I thought you'd be angry, that…er… somehow you'd blame me for this development,' Claire heard herself admit in a strained undertone.

'What use would anger be to us now?' Raif quipped as he held the door open for her to pass by him. 'One man's adversity is another man's opportunity.'

'That's a truly mature outlook you have,' she remarked, walking into a dining room with a smartly set table. 'You know… I could have made us lunch.'

'Eileen would have been offended. She owned her own restaurant before she came to work here. She's more of a caretaker than a housekeeper as I only occasionally use the

house. She found full-time retirement boring,' he explained.

'You employ a lot of people.'

'Yes. And I'm always surrounded and
rarely alone,' he agreed comfortably. 'I have
learned to adapt to that. When I was a boy,
though, I hated it.'

Claire sighed as a colourful salad was set
in front of her. 'And I ruined your moment
of escape on the beach.'

'In return you gave me an exceptional experience.'

Claire went pink and studied him anx-
iously. 'You don't have to put on a front
about how you really feel about this. I can
take the truth. I thought you'd blame me.'

'Why would I blame you? We took the
risk together and it was a risk too far,' Raif
conceded. 'But neither one of us was in the
mood to be sensible and weigh the potential
consequences.'

The light meal was exactly what her too
sensitive tummy needed. Raif received a
call, which he stepped out of the room to
take. He reappeared with a smile.

'Circe has come around from the surgery
and is doing well. I can take you back to

spend a few minutes with her before we go for our appointment.'

Claire stood, wreathed in smiles, her relief written across her face.

Raif's own mood had lightened considerably with that news. Her suspicion, however, that he was putting on a front had been perfectly correct. While he preferred honesty, diplomacy had taught him that honesty was not always wise in sensitive circumstances. He did not blame her, he blamed himself much more. He was older, more sophisticated and he had known that she was vulnerable in her grief.

If he had not been able to walk away, he should have simply acted like a friend and given her the company she needed. He should have withstood her appeal, stood firm against that outrageously seductive sense of intimacy that he had never felt with a woman before. Now they were both trapped in a bind that would inevitably force them into marriage. He saw no other possible way to extricate them both with the credit that would also give their child what he or she deserved.

They left the villa in the same limousine and returned to the veterinary surgery. Raif stood by while Claire gently stroked her bleary-eyed pet, who now had a cast enclosing one leg. A sleepy tail moved lethargically in acknowledgement.

'The vet said that she's a young cat and should heal well but that there is still a risk of seizures from the head injury, so it would be best if she remains here until she is stronger.'

'There's going to be the most ginormous bill for her treatment—' Claire began, stricken, back in the limousine.

'Claire…we have more important matters to worry about than that,' Raif pointed out drily. 'I wish it had been possible to punish the woman who hurt her, but I do believe it was an unfortunate accident. She didn't mean to hurt the animal, only to get it away from her. And in any case, the gossip will cause her a good deal of embarrassment.'

Her brow furrowed. 'Gossip?'

'Too many people witnessed the incident for it to remain unreported. She's a celebrity and someone will talk about it and rumours travel. Many people like animals and many will judge her for the injury she caused to your pet.'

Claire said nothing because she felt responsible for what had happened, feeling that she should have known better than to let the confident, independent Circe roam as she pleased on the luxury boat.

They were ushered into a private waiting room at the obstetrician's surgery. She was taken off first for a blood test and a preliminary examination with Mr Laurent. They waited for a little while before both being invited back in to see the older man again. He confirmed her pregnancy and offered her an ultrasound.

'Is there anything that can actually be seen this early?' Raif asked with a frown.

'You'll be surprised. Do you want to know the gender?'

'Yes.' Claire got up on the examination couch and the ultrasound technician helped her bare her stomach, which was relatively easy with the stretchy waistband of the trousers she wore.

'I'll be able to forward the blood-test results to you within a couple of days and that will tell you whether you're having a girl or a boy,' Mr Laurent informed them.

Raif refused a seat and hovered tautly beside her as the wand was moved over her tummy.

Her mouth running dry, Claire stilled as the three-dimensional image formed on the big screen and she quite clearly saw a baby shape, a little face, little hands, little feet. Her heart sounded very loud in her ears.

'There's your child,' she was told.

'My child…' Raif whispered in such an impressed tone that he actually stole her attention, which had been locked to the picture on the screen of the baby.

'Congratulations,' the older man told them cheerfully.

She was told that tiredness and nausea were normal in the first trimester.

'I will be very careful with Claire and our child,' Raif asserted squarely, trying to be disciplined about the image he had been shown but, in truth, he was utterly entranced by what he had seen. 'I only wish we didn't have to wait so many months until we can meet him or her.'

Claire stared at him in even greater surprise, but he was still staring at the first copy of the ultrasound, which he had intercepted on its way to her hand. 'Come on, *share*!' she urged him, reaching for it.

Having gazed in smiling fascination at the image, he handed it over with reluctance. 'I think I must like babies,' he commented.

'Don't you know?'

'No, I've only seen my brother's little girls once or twice and they were older, not infants,' he told her. 'And few of my friends have either married or started a family.'

'We're in the wrong age bracket for this,' she muttered uneasily then as they climbed back into the limousine. 'I have only one friend with children…she got married straight out of school.'

Claire pondered her distant relationship with her own surviving family members, her half-brother and her stepmother. She remained in touch with both but her relationship with her stepmother would never be anything other than strained. It struck her as very sad that she would not be able to give her child loving parents. It seemed to her then that history could sometimes repeat itself in the worst ways. She hadn't enjoyed loving parents, and neither would her baby, although at least her baby would have a loving mother, she reasoned.

'We will cope,' Raif intoned with assurance.

She wanted to query his use of that word, 'we', but decided to say nothing until he had outlined his intentions towards her and their unborn child. His unhidden interest in the baby and her welfare had, however, impressed her. Not that he was going to have much opportunity to enquire into her welfare until the yacht returned to the UK, she reflected wryly. She did hope that she wasn't going to be forced to argue with him about her ability to continue her work as an assistant chef. She wanted a good reference from Gregoire to add to her CV because it was now all the more important that she find a decent job on her return.

'I asked for your possessions to be brought here from the *Mahnoor*,' Raif informed her, surprising her, as they walked back into the white villa. 'Eileen will take you upstairs to your room.'

Thrown to the heights of disbelief by that startling information, Claire blinked and whirled round. 'You did...*what*?' she asked dangerously.

Raif straightened his broad shoulders and gave her a stoic appraisal. 'When you have had the chance to change, we will discuss the future on the terrace at the side of the house. Is that acceptable to you?'

Claire sucked in a calming breath, her hands clenched into angry fists by her side as she struggled to keep her temper. 'As long as discuss isn't another word for a command.'

'It is not,' Raif murmured softly. 'But understand now that I will not invite a scandal that would damage our child's future prospects in life. It is my duty to protect you *both* from that threat.'

And it was as though Raif had decided to suddenly drop the Mr Nice Guy façade. That cool, strong dark gaze locked to her was unexpectedly intimidating, as was the harder set of his lean, darkly handsome features. Claire paled and, turning on her heel, she joined the older woman waiting to show her upstairs. She could hardly have a fight with him in the hall in front of a witness, she reasoned unhappily. Everything they had to discuss was far too private for that.

Eileen showed her into a large and opulent bedroom. Her case was sitting ready to unpack on the bed, the bag of her pet's belongings set by a wall. Claire practised deep breathing for a minute to get a grip on her heaving emotions. How had she been naïve enough to assume that she could return to work on his yacht as an employee when she was pregnant with his child? Of course, he would not take the smallest risk of *that* news leaking into the public domain. She supposed he had to be a person of interest to the media, a VIP, the type of rich, titled single man who featured in gossip columns. She reminded herself that he had been genuinely concerned about that video clip she had taken of him undressing on the beach. He actively avoided any kind of public exposure. Did he think she might talk to someone and let the secret out? she wondered worriedly.

She pulled a dress out of her case and her toiletries and went into the en suite bathroom, helplessly awestruck by her luxury surroundings and feeling slightly guilty about the fact because only the greatest fluke had brought her into Raif's life. Had she not been in that cove at that time that one particular day, they would never even have met. The acknowledgement was oddly chilling and she wasn't quite sure why.

After a quick shower, she felt calmer and was counting her blessings, no longer fuming about the future that was being reorganised without recourse to her wishes. She had been foolish to think that she could go back to the yacht as though nothing had changed. Everything had changed and it had changed without warning. But the father of her child *was* being supportive and that was a big positive in such a situation. She simply needed to respect his sensitivities as well.

Raif watched as Claire walked out hesitantly onto the terrace. A simple cotton dress in a daisy pattern floated round her slender thighs. It occurred to him that his father would have choked at the sight of a woman's bare legs and that his brothers' wives dressed as though time had stopped fifty years ago to satisfy his father's outdated notions. Raif smiled, thoroughly entranced by Claire's sheer natural loveliness, sunlight gleaming off her fair hair.

Eileen brought out the drinks he had requested. Claire accepted a glass with an uncertain look.

'Mocktails, no alcohol,' Raif explained.

'Oh.' Claire grinned and sipped, scrutinising him below the veil of her lashes, heartbeat quickening.

He had changed as well, but only into another suit.

'Do you ever wear jeans?' she asked. 'Or shorts?'

'Occasionally. But I'm usually working and meeting people and formal apparel is expected.'

'So…' Claire compressed her lips. 'You don't want me to return to my work on the yacht to finish the trip. Is that because you think I might talk and tell people about us? I wouldn't. I may have been a chatterbox when we were together on the island, but I do know when to hold my tongue.'

'I believe that,' Raif replied soothingly. 'But where my family and my country are concerned, I am careful not to cause any scandal and now that we have a baby to consider, I have even stronger reasons for ensuring that no questionable rumours about either of us can circulate.'

'I won't tell anyone who the father of my baby is,' Claire promised him abruptly.

'That won't work, Claire. For my family to accept my son or daughter, he or she must be born within marriage. My child will never be accepted otherwise,' Raif murmured grimly. 'Nobody is more old-school than my father and what he decrees rules the whole family.'

'Because he's King,' Claire gathered, saddened to learn that her child would be denied acceptance by Raif's family on the basis of illegitimate birth.

'And because he has the power to make life very difficult for anyone who challenges him or his convictions. Quristan, however, is not an old-fashioned country,' Raif told her with perceptible pride. 'But within the palace walls, life goes on in much the same way as it did when my father was born seventy odd years ago.'

'I'm sorry that circumstances will make it impossible for our child to know your family because I really don't have any family on my side to offer,' Claire confided ruefully. 'I have a friendly enough relationship with my younger half-brother, Tom, but we're not close.'

Raif rested stunning dark golden eyes on her troubled face. 'I want you to marry me, Claire.'

Claire's eyes widened. 'You can't mean that!'

'I want you to become my wife and give our child the best possible start in life and a future that he or she is free to choose,' Raif intoned, ignoring that exclamation. 'We must not allow our impetuosity to deprive our child of the many advantages that our marriage would bring.'

Claire swallowed hard. 'You're serious,' she finally registered. 'But it would be insane.'

'We need that marriage certificate for our *baby's* sake, not for our own,' Raif pointed out. 'The ceremony would take place at the Quristani embassy in Spain. I hold diplomatic status, which makes it easier to override the usual formalities. We can be married within days…if you are willing to agree?'

Her knees were wobbling, shock winging through her, and she backed down into a seat. 'It would be insane,' she repeated weakly.

CHAPTER FIVE

'THEN I MUST be insane,' Raif countered with calm, measured diction. 'Because at this moment marriage is what I want most. It will right the wrong that we would otherwise be inflicting on our child.'

'But marriage,' Claire almost whispered. 'That's a drastic measure.'

'It need not be. If you want nothing more to do with me on a personal basis that is acceptable too,' Raif informed her tautly. 'I will ask nothing more from you than that you go through a ceremony of marriage with me.'

'You mean…we sort of fake it?' Claire looked even more dismayed by that suggestion.

'If you wish to walk away from me after the birth of our child, I will do nothing to prevent you from reclaiming your freedom,' he extended, appreciating that she still didn't grasp what he was suggesting. 'It does not have to be a for ever and ever marriage. We do not have to share a bed if you do not wish to do so. I am trying to pitch the marriage idea in terms that you will find satisfactory, but I don't know your terms.'

It crossed Claire's troubled mind that really the only thing she wanted in marriage was *him*. Not his money, not the security he offered, not some fake deal to legitimise their child. But he wasn't offering her himself on any terms. She noticed that. She noticed that the *one* thing he wasn't offering her was the chance to see if their marriage could turn into a real relationship. Clearly that wasn't on the table and why would it be? she scolded herself.

She was a chef and he was a royal prince. His background was pedigreed and rich and privileged while she was from an ordinary home with a dash of scandal in her family tree. Of course, Raif saw no prospect of his ever feeling anything more for her than he had felt the day they had first met. He had walked away from her. He hadn't texted, hadn't done anything and he was in a blasted big yacht and in charge of everywhere it went. He *could* have seen her again had he so desired. And the lowering, hurtful truth was that he *hadn't* so desired.

'You have to tell me what *you* want,' Raif prompted gently.

'I want to give my child the best I can and if that means marriage, naturally I'll consider the idea. But I don't want to fake anything. I don't think I'd be very good at that.'

'So, what *do* you want?'

Claire winced and sipped her mocktail to occupy her trembling hands because she was all worked up. 'Obviously you want a temporary marriage that will only last as long as you need it to last,' she dared to state. 'But it just seems wrong…to use holy matrimony like that, but I understand that you see it as a marriage certificate and nothing else.'

'And that makes you uncomfortable,' Raif slotted in. 'It could be as real a marriage as you want to make it and last as long as it needs to for our child's benefit.'

'How can you go from one idea to something so totally different?' Claire pressed in sincere bewilderment.

'This is a negotiation in which both of

us must compromise to some extent,' Raif pointed out. 'Basically, I will give you whatever you want if you agree to make me your legally wedded husband.'

'Then it could be a proper marriage,' Claire assumed, showing the very first tiniest, wariest hint of enthusiasm.

'And in a proper marriage, I would be able to have regular and easy access to my child, which is why I would agree to it,' Raif told her truthfully. 'I definitely don't want to be only an occasional visitor in my child's life. I would also have no objection at all to acquiring a very beautiful, sexy wife on a less temporary basis.'

Claire had turned pink. 'Sometimes you use an awful lot of words to say simple things.'

'I still want you,' Raif admitted more frankly.

'I'm not sure I can believe that when you walked away and never got in touch again,' Claire said baldly.

'There was a reason for that…' Raif compressed his lips.

'One night was enough?' Claire suggested flatly, shrugging her slim shoulders in an effort to deny her sensitivity on that score. She was embarrassed for herself because she had taken the dialogue in a direction that was too personal and revealing.

'I was very tempted to see you again, but it wouldn't have been fair to you.' Raif breathed in deep and slow, hesitating because he was not an insensitive guy. 'I'm not convinced that you truly want to hear me being *this* honest.'

'If we can't be honest even now, what kind of marriage could we have?'

'I'm in love with another woman. I fell for her many years ago,' he confessed with grim reluctance. 'But she is not someone I have ever been with or ever could be with because she is married to another man and seems perfectly happy with him.'

'There's been no affair?' Claire checked with a horrid hollow sensation spreading in her tummy.

'That was never an option…it would not be my style, nor would it be hers.'

'If it's someone you can never be with and you recognise that, you *should* have got over her by now,' Claire opined with strong conviction.

'Do you think I haven't tried?'

'Try harder,' Claire instructed with a brittle smile of encouragement, because the little hopes and dreams she had been on the brink of nourishing about his marriage proposition had just been snuffed out and stamped into dust. In love for years with an unobtainable woman? How was she supposed to fight that? *Live* with that? But then he was suggesting marriage for their child's sake and she was getting far too involved in much more personal feelings, feelings she shouldn't have and could hardly share with him. 'But thanks for telling me the truth.'

'But where does it leave us?' Raif enquired a shade drily.

'With a better understanding of each other, I hope. I assume we're staying here tonight?'

Raif nodded, trying and for once failing to read her shuttered face.

Claire was already engaged in burying his confession deep at the back of her mind. Reassured that there had been no affair and that he believed he could never be with the woman of his dreams, she told herself that she shouldn't be hurt by the unavailability of his heart. What was more, she did respect him for telling her an ugly truth, which no woman would welcome. 'I was going to ask you to let me sleep on my decision, but I don't think that's necessary now. I'll marry you.'

'I won't give you cause to regret it.'

'You have to be faithful and honest,' she told him ruefully. 'That is all I ask from you. I also don't *ever* want to know the identity of the woman you told me about. Let's be clear about that point.'

Raif released his breath in a slow hiss. 'I can meet those terms. Then we have a deal.'

'No, *not* a deal, a marriage. You're too much of a businessman sometimes,' she reproved.

Raif grinned with appreciation of that criticism, enjoying the way she treated him: hiding nothing, pretending nothing, indeed disdaining pretence. There was much he admired about Claire that went way beyond her physical appearance and her effect on his libido. Looking at her, he was aroused, fiercely aroused, at the awareness that soon they would be married and she would be his again. When she married him, together they would be able to give their child a sta-

ble, loving home. He did not want anything
fake either, any more than he wanted to contemplate a future divorce. Divorce, after all,
had ripped his life and his mother's asunder,
as well as separating him from his brothers and his father. He would not allow their
child to suffer such cruel losses and mercifully the answer to preventing that risk was
in his own hands. If he made Claire happy,
she would not seek a divorce.

They had a late supper on the terrace, and
it was magical, fairy lights twinkling over
the trees, apparently left over from some
fancy business dinner he had once held at
the villa. His reserve was back squarely in
the control of him by then. Personal questions still made him tense. He did admit
barely knowing his father in any other guise
than as the King at ceremonial events. She
made him laugh when she told him about
being forced to join the church choir as a
child even though she had the harsh singing
voice of a corncrake. He frowned, though,
when she mentioned being loudly rebuked
by her father from the pulpit when she whispered or squirmed in her pew as a little girl
at Sunday service.

She went up to bed with a little knot of sadness locked up inside her heart. If he hadn't told her about his love for another woman, she knew she would have crept out of her own bed to find his, but such boldness no longer felt possible. Yes, he still might want her in the most basic way of all, but pride warned her that he should also learn to appreciate her for other things. What exactly those other things might be, well, she had no very clear idea, but somehow slipping covertly into bed with Raif in a way that once would have felt utterly natural and normal to her no longer felt so straightforward.

Claire wasn't someone accustomed to hiding her emotions and she was used to acting on them, but intelligence told her that in the future she would have to be more guarded, even if it was just in an attempt to match Raif. A princess wouldn't have an unruly tongue, a silly giggle or think of fluffy, flirty stuff like putting on fancy underwear with which to shock him. And he would be shocked because he had finally admitted that that night he had been a virgin as well. She cherished that fact. At least that other woman couldn't steal *that* from her as well.

Raif went for a cold shower, but it didn't solve his problem and he decided that cold showers were very overrated. He marvelled at all the years he had remained impervious to such cravings. Now he craved Claire as much as though she were some illicit drug already in his bloodstream, but after the casual way their relationship had started out he was convinced that he ought to treat her with the greatest possible respect to ensure that she did not think he would ever take her beautiful body for granted.

In the morning, Claire asked what she should wear for the wedding ceremony and Raif frowned. 'I'll consult my staff and organise something here at the house. You will require a complete wardrobe, but we can't shop together here in Monaco where I am well known.'

He didn't want to hurt Claire by telling her the truth that if his father found out that he was marrying a woman without his approval he would move heaven and earth to stop him because Claire was neither royal nor connected to some important Quristani family. At the same time, however, his father had never once indicated any interest in when or even if Raif would ever get married, although he had exerted himself to personally select his older sons' wives. Having consulted his lawyer, Raif knew there was nothing in the constitution that even implied that he needed anyone's permission to marry and once the deed was done, it was done. He would not risk his child being born out of wedlock.

Claire went to visit Circe again, but this time with Mohsin as her escort. Her cat was more responsive than she had been the day before and Claire was glad, because it looked unlikely now that her pet would suffer any further problems from her injuries. She regretted her inability to take Circe back to the villa with her, but that wasn't possible when they were about to fly to Spain, and she could hardly saddle Eileen with a convalescent cat.

'So, what do I wear?' Claire asked Raif again when on her return he informed her the 'fashion people' had arrived and awaited her in the main salon. 'A wedding dress or something less bridal?'

'That is immaterial. We will not be visible once we arrive at the embassy. You will like our ambassador and his wife there. I went to school with Kashif, and Stella is English, like you,' he told her cheerfully.

'I would like a wedding dress,' Claire admitted.

'Claire...' Raif traced a long finger across her anxious and downcurved lips, troubled by her uncertainty. '*Smile*. I don't care if you dress up like a pirate. I only care that we take this important step together.'

Claire quivered and smiled so brightly that he smiled as well. And, heavens, he was so beautiful to her in that moment that she almost stretched up to kiss him. The smouldering glow in his tortoiseshell eyes lit her up like a firework inside herself where it didn't show, and her thighs pressed tight together to contain the lingering hollow ache of longing. She wanted him as she had never wanted him before, even more than she had wanted him the first time, because now she knew what he could do to her with his mouth, his hands and his body. Blinking rapidly, she forced herself to turn away.

The 'fashion people' were a stylist and representatives of several designer salons, each vying with the other to fulfil her requirements. She was measured, shown pictures to establish her likes and dislikes and, in a whirl of activity and useful advice, was promised a dream wardrobe that would suit both hot and cool climates. She knew that within months most of the apparel wouldn't fit her but, mindful of the need for discretion, she didn't mention the fact that she was pregnant. And she was downright excited at having picked her dream wedding gown, grateful that her tummy was still flat for the occasion while inwardly apologising to the baby she carried for her ridiculous vanity.

The next day, Raif handed her his phone and explained that it was the obstetrician on the line with her test results. Tensing, Claire wandered across the terrace and listened as the sex of her child was shared. She handed back the phone.

'We're having a boy!' she proclaimed with a smile.

Raif grinned. 'I truly didn't mind which,' he confessed. 'But perhaps because I'm a boy, having a boy as a first child seems an easier prospect.'

Forty-eight hours later, they moved separately through the airport and ignored each other in the VIP lounge. 'It was like being a spy!' Claire told Raif in delight when he finally boarded his private jet to join her. 'And Mohsin is like a shadow when he moves around. I loved it. I was careful not to even *look* in your direction!'

'You are a very good sport, Claire,' he countered with a helpless grin. 'Most women would kill me for forcing them to hide on their wedding day!'

'I'm not most women.'

'I know that very well.'

It was true that the fabulous clothes that had begun arriving the day after her consultation with the fashionistas had given Claire more confidence than she had ever had before. There was a newly discovered pleasure in knowing that she looked her very best in an elegant dress the colour of cinnamon, teamed with toning shoes and a stylish bag.

They landed in Barcelona and travelled separately to the embassy where she would put on her wedding gown. The embassy was a big, tall, classical stone building behind secure walls, and she climbed out of the limo to be shown indoors, where she was greeted by a young brunette with a bubbly personality.

'I'm Kashif's wife, Stella,' she announced. 'This is so exciting!'

'Yes, isn't it?' Claire agreed, relaxed by that greeting from someone she reckoned was only a few years older and happy to follow Stella up an imposing staircase into an elegant bedroom where her luggage already awaited her.

'I can't wait to see the dress!' Stella confided. 'I think it's awful, though, that Raif feels like he has to get married in secret just because of that old dictator of a father!'

Alerted to the fact that her hostess had no idea she was pregnant, Claire resisted a smile at the full extent of her future husband's reserve even with a personal friend and his wife. Only as the rest of that speech sank in did the urge to smile die altogether. So, that was the *real* reason for the secrecy, she registered in dismay. Obviously, understandably, Raif was taking a wife of whom his father would not approve. Resolving not to feel wounded by that reality, she whisked her dress out of the cloaking garment bag that had enclosed it and dug out the rest of her bridal outfit.

'No man deserves to be loved more than Raif,' Stella told her, seating herself on the edge of the bed. 'He had an awful childhood and he'll never tell you about it.'

Claire wrinkled her nose. 'He's very reserved but we're all different, aren't we?'

'Do you want to know the facts?'

'I could know already,' she pointed out. 'I know the basics…his parents' divorce, his mother's depression. But I don't think I'm entitled to know anything he hasn't chosen to tell me.'

'Sorry, removing foot that I had inserted in mouth!' Stella commented with a guilty giggle. 'You're loyal. He's never had that either, someone loyal to *him*. He's too busy being loyal and respectful to a family that act like he barely exists, except when it suits them to recognise him. They only invite him to official events. He got left out of all the weddings, new births and family celebrations.'

'He's a very special guy,' Claire muttered helplessly, hurt that Raif had to endure such poor treatment from the family who should have been closest to him.

Of course, was she really one to talk? Her own childhood had been no walk in the park. Her father and her stepmother had raised her without affection or praise of any kind. Even so, nobody had beat her, nobody had starved her and, for those reasons, she didn't feel that she had that much ground for complaint when others went through much worse experiences. It had been rather distressing to appreciate as a teenager that her father didn't even appear to like her and only seemed to look at her to find fault. Of course, she had reminded him of her mother, having the same hair colour and eyes, but that didn't excuse him, in her opinion, for punishing her for his ex-wife's choices. Perhaps Raif was paying the same price as she had for *his* resemblance to *his* mother!

'You *care* about him,' Stella murmured with warm approval. 'That's all I really wanted to know.'

Claire reddened as she undressed. She could have asked for privacy, but she would never manage to get into her romantic confection of satin organza without female assistance. It was a designer gown with tight lace sleeves and a sweetheart neckline, the bodice neat and fitted and the skirt narrow and long. It was the colour of pale sepia, the shade that most suited her skin tone, and the shape flattered her curves without showing too much skin. The fabric was scattered with seed pearls.

'Raif had his mother's jewellery brought here from London for your use,' Stella informed her. 'There's enough in that chest to sink the *Titanic*.'

'He didn't mention it.' Claire climbed into her gown and eased her hands into the sleeves while Stella helped to untangle the skirt. Righting the shoulders, Claire straightened.

'It's really beautiful.' Stella sighed as she proceeded to close the back of the gown. 'We had a civil wedding. I wore a suit. If I'd my time over again, I'd wear a wedding dress.'

Claire dug her feet into her ridiculously fancy wedding shoes with pleasure and approached the giant chest by the wall. 'The jewellery is in here?'

The chest was filled with boxes. Claire flipped a lid on the largest box on top and gasped at the rainbow reflections of the diamonds.

'That necklace is perfect for your neckline,' her companion declared.

The diamond necklace and the earrings that matched were donned.

'There must be a tiara in here, more than one, I would assume. She *was* a queen.'

'A tiara would be over the top for me,' Claire demurred.

'But not for a princess and Raif has organised a photographer,' Stella warned her, surprising her in turn.

A tiara was indeed located with ease and Claire allowed her companion to anchor it above the short veil at the back of her head. Nerves clogged her throat as she surveyed her reflection because, with all those diamonds and clad in her dream gown, she barely recognised herself. That disturbing title 'Princess' struck her as more threatening than something to which she might have aspired because she knew herself to be absolutely ordinary in every way.

They went downstairs into a large room where Raif and two other men awaited them. As she was introduced to Stella's husband,

Kashif, and the minister present to perform their ceremony, Claire only had eyes for Raif, resplendent in a morning suit, a pearl-grey cravat at his throat to match the cummerbund round his narrow waist, a custom-made jacket with a tail outlining his splendid physique. He looked amazing, she thought. Well, he always looked amazing, but he contrived to look especially amazing in that garb, his black hair gleaming above his stunning eyes, his strong jawline freshly shaven, framing his wide, sensual mouth. For an instant, she really couldn't credit that he was about to marry *her*. He reached for her hand with his easy smile and led her over to the table that had been topped with a giant floral arrangement. He looked down at her as though she were the only woman in the world.

It was a short and sweet ceremony, but Claire listened to every word and exchanged rings with Raif in breathless wonder that they were actually becoming man and wife.

Raif studied her with mesmerising dark golden eyes. In that highly feminine dress, she was every dream woman he had ever had and Kashif had done everything he had asked him and more in preparation for their wedding. Sadly for Claire's sake, there were only two guests, he acknowledged, but there had to be some drawbacks to a secret event.

'That was wonderful,' she told him brightly as their hosts led them to the rear garden with its ornamental box-hedged flowerbeds for the photographer to take advantage of the setting.

'You look fantastic,' Raif whispered only loud enough for her to hear.

More colour warmed her already flushed cheeks and her blue eyes sparkled with pleasure. 'I wasn't expecting a Christian minister and ceremony,' she whispered back.

'I wanted you to be comfortable,' Raif responded.

And she ate sparingly of the delicious dinner that followed because she was lost in a reverie. There had never been a man in her life, including her late father, who had worried so much about what would make *her* happy. She had never enjoyed such thoughtful consideration. Yet Raif had had her injured cat treated and had had Claire ferried back and forth on pet visits, which others might reasonably have deemed unnecessary. He had ensured she had new clothes for her future role, and he had even had his late mother's jewellery collection offered to her for use. Yet he made no demands on her whatsoever.

She decided that he was the most unselfish person she had ever met and that melted her heart, because there could be few men as rich and in possession of a superyacht who, in his position, would have made so much silent, kind effort on her behalf. And he always brushed away any attempt to thank him.

'You've made it a wonderful day,' she murmured.

'That was the goal,' he confided with satisfaction.

Below the table, she rested a hand on a lean thigh and petted him as though he were a cat, unable to express her gratitude in any other way. His hand came down briefly over hers and then shifted again and she took the hint and retrieved her own. No, Raif was never ever going to be demonstrative in front of others, she reflected fondly. No PDAs from him!

Claire knew that she was already halfway in love with the man she had married. She had never met a man like him, never dreamt he could even exist, and now here she was with his wedding ring on her finger, and she could not believe that fortune had smiled on her to such an extent. Mentally she was listing his every plus and those pluses just kept on mounting in number.

Raif was thinking that even the touch of her tiny hand on his thigh was too much for him to bear. He was already as hard as a rock. He wanted to defy every civil, social tenet to snatch her away somewhere private where he could *touch* her. He had genuinely not appreciated that one foray into the world of sex would leave him so agonisingly needy because in every other field he was very controlled, very cool and unfailingly practical. Claire, however, punched buttons he hadn't known he had. Just a smile, a bright glance from those eyes of hers, the peachy pout of her lips when she laughed, and she laughed frequently, unlike most of the people he knew. Being with Claire felt vaguely to him like being in the sunshine all the time, where all the usual things that worried him miraculously vanished.

It was after ten that evening when Raif smoothly extracted them from their hosts' convivial company. He explained that they would be spending the night in the suite of rooms created for his father at the embassy when he first became King. As a young man King Jafri had happily travelled abroad.

'And then there was apparently some kind of scandal with a young woman that had to be hushed up and he never left Quristan again,' Raif informed her wryly, opening a door into a large formal drawing room. 'It soured him on travel, foreigners and tourists as well.'

'Not a forgiving person,' Claire gathered as he opened the door into the most grandiose bedroom she had ever seen.

A gilded four-poster bed, garnished with scarlet and gold drapes, sat on a polished dais at the far end of the room, rather resembling something that she thought might have featured in a big-budget royal film. 'Oh, my goodness…are *we* going to spend the night in that monstrosity?' She gasped.

'Yes, it is a monstrosity, isn't it?' Raif agreed with humour, relieved it wasn't only him who found his father's taste for medieval splendour weird in modern times. 'But this is where I have to sleep when I stay here. Kashif tells me that it's an exact replica of my father's bed in the palace. I've never been in his wing of the palace, so I wouldn't know.'

Claire was reminded by that remark that he had been denied a close relationship with his surviving parent. That he had never seen his father's private quarters said it all.

'Do you want anything to drink?' Raif enquired, hovering beside the drinks cabinet.

'No, thanks. After that elaborate meal, I'm full,' she quipped, moving over to the ornate gilded dresser to begin removing her diamond jewellery.

'We're leaving first thing in the morning to spend a few days alone in the Alpujarra.'

'I wasn't expecting a honeymoon,' she told him. 'And I never thanked you for offering me these beautiful pieces to wear today.'

'I inherited my mother's jewellery and, as my bride, you're entitled to wear the pieces,' Raif countered. 'Do you need some help?'

'I'm afraid you're likely to have to unwrap me like a parcel tonight,' Claire muttered shyly as she struggled to undo the necklace.

'Let me…' Cool fingers brushed her nape as he opened the clasp and laid the necklace down on the dresser.

Claire removed the earrings and turned back to him, colour in her cheeks at the silence spreading round them.

Raif extended a wrapped gift box to her. 'It's a wedding present from me.'

'I didn't get you anything!' Claire wailed in immediate dismay.

'Claire,' Raif murmured with a smouldering smile. 'My gift today was *you*!'

Claire was busy reddening and ripping open the packaging to discover the diamond-studded watch within. 'Wow, triple wow!' She gasped, suddenly short of breath as she had not been at the loan of his mother's jewellery because the watch was a personal gift for her alone. Without hesitation, she undid the serviceable chrome watch she wore to attach the new one. 'It's beautiful, Raif. Thank you very much.'

Gazing down into her smiling face, he bent down and captured her lips hungrily with his own. 'It was nothing,' he started to say, intending to say more but too drawn by the taste of her to linger on speech.

A little quiver of vibrant response ran through Claire, and she leant into that kiss like a drowning swimmer reaching for a life ring, hands closing over his shoulders, slender body sealing to the hard muscular contours of his.

CHAPTER SIX

'I NEED YOUR help to get out of this dress,' Claire mumbled against the allure of his mouth.

With effort, Raif took a step back from her, one hand already engaged in wrenching loose his cravat and cummerbund. 'We're both wearing far too many clothes.'

'Like you on the beach,' she reminded him with a smile, no lingering hurt now in the memory of him walking away the next morning. She understood him better even if she wished things weren't the way they were with him being in love with another woman. Only the conception of their child had given Raif the framework to fit her into his life as well and just at that moment she didn't resent that prosaic truth, even though she suspected that there might come a time in the future when she would be more sensitive and might well long for more.

As he doffed his jacket, she turned round to present him with the hooks and ties at the back of her gown.

'I like the subtle little opening...*here*,' he confided huskily as he traced the keyhole shape with a fingertip. 'In fact, I love the dress. It's sexy without showing anything much.'

He unhooked the bodice, unlaced the ties and she began to pull her arms out of the sleeves. 'The lingerie isn't quite so subtle,' she warned him carefully.

'What *only* I see can be as daring as you like,' Raif told her with a slashing grin. 'I may have chosen not to engage in casual flings, but I am not a prude.'

Face colouring and fully aware of his intense interest, Claire let the gown drop to her ankles to expose her thigh-high stockings and garter, matched to a white filmy silk bra and knickers adorned with blue ribbons.

'That word you use...*wow*, just about covers my appreciation,' Raif confided, colour flaring along his high cheekbones as he looked his fill at his bride, her luscious curves cupped in fine silk and lace. He embarked on his shirt buttons with alacrity.

'No, I open those,' Claire announced, stepping forward, empowered by his appreciation and still wearing her heels, to undo those buttons for him because she wasn't about to mention it *again*, but she loved the look and shape of him as well. The shirt parted on a sliver of bronzed chest and his taut, indented abdomen. He was on gym equipment every day and it showed.

As Claire tipped his shirt off his shoulders and let her hands drop to slide up over his muscular torso, Raif was mesmerised by her touch and the hunger for him in her bright blue eyes. Being desired to that extent struck him as a blessing to be savoured. The shirt dropped, he toed off his shoes and peeled off his socks without removing his attention from her for even a second.

Claire reached round to unclip her bra and his hands came up to hold hers. 'I want to do that,' he admitted. 'I want to strip you naked and live out every fantasy I've had about you over the past two months.'

Her eyes widened, she swallowed and

stilled. His husky words made her even more aware of the pool of urgent heat forming in her pelvis and the tightness of her nipples. He undid her bra and let it fall, pulling her back against him, letting his hands glide up to cup the firm curves and his thumbs catch her swollen nipples. 'I have dreamt of this,' he groaned, tugging her back against him, making her awesomely conscious of his erection.

'Can't deny having the odd recollection of that night myself,' she admitted.

'It was amazing,' Raif told her. 'But tonight will be even better.'

She spun round and unzipped his trousers, fingers delving beneath the fine weave to stroke his hard length. He shuddered against her and kissed her with unleashed hunger before dropping down on his knees in front of her and gently tugging down her knickers.

'We will take this slow tonight,' he asserted.

Naked, Claire squirmed in front of him, horribly conscious of her unclad self and every defect she had ever believed her body had. 'I'm quite happy with fast…'

'Think of yourself as a gourmet meal,' Raif advised.

'Right...' Claire gasped as he pried her thighs apart and pressed his mouth to the heart of her because she hadn't been expecting that. All the lamps were lit and she felt floodlit and embarrassed. 'We could get into the bed—'

'It looks like Count Dracula's bed.'

'He slept in a coffin,' she incised.

Raif ceased his attentions and looked up at her. 'What's wrong?'

Claire winced. 'I just feel a bit shy about standing here... I *know* it's stupid—'

Raif sprang up and lifted her up into his arms to carry her over to the bed. 'Nothing you feel is stupid. I'm afraid you're dealing with a bridegroom set on living out every sexual fantasy he ever had...and almost all of those were about you and very recent.'

Her awkwardness melted away at that admission while her spine met the cool crisp white linen beneath her. Not a scrap of shyness in his bearing, Raif peeled off his trousers and his boxers and joined her on the bed. Hot, golden, muscular flesh met hers.

He stared down at his bride in fascination,

thinking that he *finally* had a family, someone who would look to him first and a child
whom he would cherish. He had never really
had anyone of his own. Claire and their son,
however, would be wholly and absolutely *his*
and that meant a lot to a man who had pretty
much felt alone all his life.

He had loved his mother, but she had had
too many other interests with her travel, her
endless parties and affairs with unsuitable
men to spend much time with the little boy
in the nursery. And when he got older, she
had tried to make him a friend rather than
a son, which had often been very uncomfortable for him. Yet he had long understood
why his mother had only found comfort in
her life of excess: his father's rejection had
decimated her pride and when his father had
swiftly chosen a much younger beauty as a
second wife, Mahnoor had been absolutely
gutted. Her wounded ego had driven her into
the arms of other men.

'You're beautiful, Claire,' he murmured
softly, gorgeous black-lashed eyes locked to
her smile. 'And I'm incredibly happy about
our son. I'll be with you every step of the way.'

She drew him down to her, fingers sliding up into his luxuriant black hair, and his mouth crushed hers in a remarkably sensual and urgent claiming that made the blood chase through her veins faster. She arched up to him, her whole body craving his, the nagging ache pulsing at the heart of her almost unbearable to endure. As her legs wrapped round him Raif shifted against her with a roughened sound deep in his chest and sank deep into her, her body stretching to enclose him while a delicious friction burn rippled through her.

'Slow!' Raif reminded her in reproof.

And Claire laughed because he was so serious about the concept, as if they had to proceed from point A to point B to win the points and skipping a possible stage could be a hanging offence. 'No, it's win-win all the way for us the way I'm feeling.'

'I wanted it to be perfect this time,' Raif confided, his big strong body trembling over her as she shifted up to him in a quite deliberately inviting way.

Claire gazed up to his lean, dark, wonderfully handsome face and ran a thumb along the lower edge of his compressed lips. 'I think it's always perfect with you,' she murmured softly. 'I don't want to go slow *this* time. If you start treating me like an invalid here in bed as well, I'll kill you.'

An unwilling edge of amusement tugged at the corners of his unsmiling mouth. 'Is that so?'

Claire gave him another hip-tilting motion to urge him on. 'Yes, because there is no such thing as perfect when we're together. Being happy is a much better goal.'

Raif nodded and moved in a remarkably enervating way that sent the pleasure she craved winging through every sensitive nerve ending. Her head fell back because he had got the message and that was really all that mattered. Only later would she wonder if that was what Raif did to himself, held himself to some impossible, unsustainable high standard in every field of his life because someone somewhere at some stage of his growing years had made him feel as though he would never be good enough. And she understood that, because she had been made to feel the same way.

She strained up to him, her serious thoughts flying away as a new urgency gripped her. Raif was moving and every lithe thrust of his body into hers gave her so much sensation she felt as though she were drowning in the sensual waves building at the centre of her, tightening inner muscles she had not known she had, her tension rising fast. He shifted them over onto their side and slid a hand between them to find that tiny nub that controlled her and as he drove into her one last forceful time, the whole world splintered round her and she was flying high on such excitement that something uncommonly like a shriek was wrenched from her.

'Oh, my goodness, did I—?'

'Yes, and loudly, but there's nobody else to hear in this wing of the embassy because below us are the offices,' Raif told her, holding her gripped to him as if she were likely to make a sudden break for freedom. 'I'm not sure I deserve you.'

'That'll teach you not to get naked in a public place again and use your beautiful body to tempt an innocent woman into what my father would have called improper behaviour!' Claire teased, tickling his ribs because once again he looked quite ridiculously serious.

Raif started laughing. 'My father would also have found our behaviour improper but without it I wouldn't have you…and I can't bring myself to feel a single atom of regret,' he confessed ruefully. 'Even though I plunged us both into a storm of trouble.'

'It takes two to tango,' Claire reminded him, throwing off the sheet, because Raif burned much hotter than she did, and she was roasting. 'Is there any air conditioning in here?'

Raif let her go and sprang out of bed to stride back naked to the door and hit a switch. 'I always leave it off…sorry.'

'The heat doesn't usually bother me this much. It may be because I'm pregnant… or because I have a very hot guy walking naked across my bedroom floor…a very hot *aroused* guy!' she tossed at him irrepressibly, giggling at his arrested expression.

'Well, since this wedding night doesn't appear to be under my control,' Raif intoned lazily as he flung himself back on the bed, 'maybe *you* would like to tell *me* what we do next.'

'I'm not about to tell you, I'm much more likely to *show* you,' Claire declared, rolling closer to investigate every fascinating part of his body that she could see and touch.

'I like that,' he groaned at one point. 'Oh, I really, *really* like that...'

Sooner than either of them would have ideally liked, it was morning and time for a quick breakfast in their palatial suite and then departure.

'On your way back to the yacht, spend one last night here and join us for dinner,' Stella pleaded.

They flew to Almeria and completed the journey to the mountain villa by car. From the moment they stepped down onto the first paved terrace of a series, Claire was enchanted by the view of the wooded hillsides and that was even before Raif pointed out the Rock of Gibraltar and Morocco in the misty distance. A forest of pine and oak trees surrounded the wonderfully colourful lush tropical garden. High on a nearby hill and surrounded by a rambling village stood an old, ruined castle, its jagged roofline piercing the bright blue sky.

With wide eyes, Claire stared at the spectacular infinity pool complete with steps, wet bar and a miniature island, before turning on her heel to walk inside the house.

'What's wrong?' Raif followed her. 'Don't you like it?'

Claire tugged her appreciative attention from the beautiful tiled living area, patio doors open on all sides to make the most of the fabulous views, and swallowed hard in her dazed state. 'It's fantastic,' she whispered. 'How could I *not* like it? Do you own this place?'

'It's a rental but I own the company. I developed the villas in this area, a handful from scratch and others from derelict homesteads,' he explained calmly. 'I suppose I do own it, only I don't regard it as one of my private homes.'

She peered into the kitchen with its pretty blue shutters, catering-sized stove and smooth surfaces. *I suppose I do own it. One* of my private homes. She blinked and almost laughed. He had brought her into a disconcerting new world of wealth and opulence, and she could still barely credit that such a lifestyle was now hers to share with him. Her exploration continued into a stunning bedroom with a mosaic of richly coloured traditional tiles on the wall and a superb marble bathroom.

'Someone will come in every day to look after us,' Raif revealed, stilling behind her to tug her back into his arms. 'I know you would cook but you're not supposed to on your honeymoon.'

'Is that so, Your Royal Highness?' she teased, wriggling back into much-needed contact with his long, lean, powerful body, her own nerve endings flaring at that necessary physical connection. The sudden pinching of her nipples and the stirring pulse of need between her thighs were already becoming familiar to her.

'Yes, that is so,' he breathed raggedly as he backed down on the bed and flipped her to face him, large hands framing her cheeks as he tasted her lush mouth with raw, driving urgency.

'I can't wait to be inside you again,' he groaned, dazzling dark golden eyes locked to her pink face. 'I want you all the time. Every time I look at you, I end up wanting you again.'

Her reddened lips curved into a playful

grin. 'So, we didn't burn ourselves out last night, after all...'

'I can't believe I'll ever burn out on you,' Raif forecast.

'You're not allowed to wear a suit the whole time we're here,' Claire warned him bossily. 'You're here to *relax*.'

'I'm not good at relaxing.'

'But I am,' she told him brightly, unknotting his tie, embarking on his shirt buttons.

Raif took the hint with alacrity, standing up to peel off his clothing at speed.

Claire kicked off her shoes and removed her jacket to sit on the bed as if she were overseeing a strip show. 'Yes...yes...*yes*!' she told him irrepressibly, delighted by the slivers of bronzed muscular torso and hair-roughened thighs being bared.

Raif rolled his eyes. 'You're objectifying me,' he complained.

Claire tossed her head, rumpled blonde tresses flying back to expose her smile. 'But I think you *like* being appreciated by me.'

Faint colour accentuated the sculpted slant of his high cheekbones. 'You are right,' he conceded, sliding down the zip on her dress, burying his mouth in the sensitive skin between her neck and her shoulder and laughing as she gasped at the sensation.

His hands cupped her breasts as her bra fell away, catching each nipple between finger and thumb to tug at the sensitive buds. And then he was turning her over again, addressing his attention to the rest of her with glorious attention to every responsive part of her. She was wet and ready for him, arching as he drove into her with a helpless cry of delight. And the tension buzzing through her entire body reached a swift and breathless height in a hail of sensual excitement and the sweet convulsions sent her straight to sleep afterwards.

Raif shook her gently awake in the dusk light filtering through the light drapes at the window. 'Dinner will be ready for us in thirty minutes.'

'My goodness, how long have I been asleep?' Claire exclaimed, sitting up in a rush.

'Obviously you needed the rest and perhaps I should be a little more careful about overtiring you,' he murmured worriedly.

'No, I'm not listening to talk of that kind on our honeymoon!' Claire covered her ears with expressive hands in emphasis. 'Were you not in the same meeting we had with the obstetrician? It's *normal* for me to be more tired. It's all right for me to sleep more.'

'Got it,' Raif groaned, vaulting upright.

'I'm sorry. I'm just a little…touchy about being pregnant…sometimes,' she mumbled, sliding out of the bed double quick to head for the bathroom because she knew that she was only sensitive about that subject because he had married her purely because she had conceived.

That little awkward moment was forgotten over dinner on one of the terraces. Since Raif had visited the Alpujarra before, he knew the prettiest villages to visit, and plans were made for the next day. He was wearing jeans, and she was convinced that they were entirely for her benefit because they were decidedly new, and she smiled and smiled at the reflection. She listened to him talk with an abstracted expression, admiring the sound of his voice, his lean, strong face, his truly stunning eyes and the length of his lashes, even his gestures once he relaxed and began to use his hands to express himself more.

Yes, she was falling for the guy she'd married, falling head over heels over common sense but there didn't seem to be much she could do about it. And why would she want to change her feelings anyway? After all, they had married for the long haul, not merely to legitimise the birth of their baby son, she reminded herself soothingly. All the same, had she had better control over her emotions she would have chosen to slow down the development of those feelings because that would have been more sensible. Falling madly in love so fast with a guy who loved someone else was kind of scary, because she knew she was leaving herself wide open to being hurt. What if he got bored with her? What if he decided he wasn't happy with her? How would she feel then, when she had already given him her all?

Over the following week, they slowly became inseparable. Raif kept on warning her that he would need to do some work, but he never got to grips with leaving her alone for long enough to accomplish much and Claire had no objections to make. They explored the Moorish ruined castle on the hill, wandered through the picturesque village full of whitewashed houses, a charming little church, and she began to browse handicraft shops obsessively. By the time they had finished touring the local villages, she had become the proud owner of three colourful hand-woven Alpujarra rugs, a couple of baskets and several ceramic items. There was a trip to an artisan chocolatier, a picnic within view of a glorious waterfall, which they had walked to, Raif thankfully keeping any misgivings about the effect of too much exercise on her fecund condition to himself.

And she cooked because he couldn't keep her out of the kitchen, no matter how hard he tried. She made all the dishes she loved, with the added extra of local almonds, figs, honey and cheese.

For their last evening at the villa, Raif had made special plans. He had organised private access to the Alhambra complex. At sunset the ancient Moorish buildings glowed pink. As one of the best surviving historic palaces in the Islamic world, it was of particular interest to Raif, who had visited several times before. There was no need for a tour guide as he showed her around. He explained the irrigation system to her and told her that there was a similar arrangement of aqueducts and water channels in the Old Palace in Quristan. He translated the poetry on the walls for her and then urged her outside again where a table and two chairs awaited them beside a tranquil pool that reflected them like a still mirror.

'We're actually going to dine here?' she exclaimed in sheer wonder, her head turning as a small flamenco group sat down several yards away and began to play evocative Spanish guitar music, the singer's atmospheric voice soaring soulfully into the night air. 'This is amazing, Raif. When did you arrange all this?'

'At the start of the week. I wanted you to have a special memory for our last day,' Raif proffered, shrugging off her astonishment as a meal was served to them by uniformed waiters while their security team fanned round the edges of open space.

'It will be a beautiful memory for ever,' Claire declared, with over-hormonal tears prickling the backs of her eyes, but she was resisting an urge to stand up and hug him, which she knew he would dislike with an audience.

The following day they packed for the return to Barcelona and arrived early evening to a chirpy welcome from Stella and a quieter greeting from Kashif. They dined with the other couple, sat up late over coffee and went to bed in the grand four-poster that still made them laugh.

Someone was banging on the door and a phone was buzzing incessantly somewhere. Claire opened her eyes on complete darkness and knew it was the middle of the night and she experienced that intense sense of something being wrong. It made her fumble to light a bedside lamp and shake Raif awake.

He came awake and was alert much faster than she was. He vaulted straight out of bed to head for the door stark naked.

'Clothes, Raif!' she called, scrambling out of bed to race into the bathroom and yank a towelling robe off the hook and throw it to him. He put it on in haste, knotted the sash and went straight to the door.

She heard Kashif's voice, but he was speaking in their language, not in English. She slid hurriedly out of bed and began rooting for a robe. Then as Raif came back inside, pale, his features oddly tight and expressionless, she decided just by looking at his face to put on clothes instead.

'Something's happened…a car accident in Quristan, family involved. I need to get dressed and go downstairs,' he framed flatly. 'Kashif is breaking the bad news in little nuggets to keep me calm. I know him of old.'

'I'm so sorry, Raif,' Claire whispered. 'What can I do to help?'

'Nothing if what I suspect is true.' He sighed and by that she registered that, apparently, he was already convinced that someone had died. His father? An accident though? From what she understood his father was more likely to pass away from ill health and old age. Her brow furrowing in a frown, she went into her suitcase to find her clothes, choosing trousers and a light top.

She felt as though the world had stopped turning without warning and flung her off into frightening freefall. They had had a wonderful wedding day and an even more incredible week together at the mountain villa. She was happier than she had ever thought to be in her entire life and now she had one of those sixth-sense creeping suspicions that that was all about to fall apart before she could even get to enjoy it. A sense of doom, she registered unhappily. Why wrap it up?

Raif went for a quick shower and emerged to dress, choosing, she noticed, a business suit and a plain white shirt, stuffing a dark tie into one pocket as if he didn't yet have the heart to put it on.

'Shall I come downstairs with you?' Claire asked hesitantly. 'I should.'

'No, this is for me to deal with. I don't want you getting upset about anything,' Raif informed her levelly, his seeming confidence in that necessity overruling every personal feeling.

'I was thinking of you…maybe wanting company,' Claire almost whispered, not knowing how to sensitively say that she was unlikely to get upset on anyone's account but *his* when his family were all strangers to her.

Raif shook his handsome dark head, already walking towards the door, spine rigid, shoulders squared as though he were already preparing himself for the worst possible news.

And tears stung Claire's eyes as the door closed in his wake because she now felt that she had somehow failed in the first duty of being a wife. In such a situation, he needed support as well, but she could hardly force her company on him. Sadly, their marriage was too new for that, and she couldn't afford to make assumptions and push the point because undoubtedly there *were* people who preferred to deal with such matters alone. And it was perfectly possible that her presence would be more of an added stress factor than a comfort because he could never forget for long that she was in a delicate condition, even though she didn't feel the slightest bit delicate.

Ten minutes later, Stella arrived in the sitting room beyond the bedroom with a laden tray, containing tea and snacks, her bubbly personality muted in contrast to her liveliness over dinner the night before. 'I guessed you'd be up and pacing. I would be too,' she said, pursing her lips.

Claire took charge of the tea and poured. 'Do you know—?'

Stella lifted both hands in a negative motion. 'No. No, I don't know who's involved. What I do know is that it's very confidential information, which came direct from the Quristani government, and when it comes to work issues, Kashif is a professional to his fingertips, even with me.'

'I wanted to be with Raif,' Claire admitted then.

Stella leant over and patted her knee consolingly. 'Of course you did, but men are stubborn and proud. Most of them don't do vulnerable if they can avoid it.'

Even though her companion talked good sense, Claire's nerves were leaping up and down inside her like jumping beans. Only good manners kept her seated beside Stella when she wanted to pace the floor and go frantic because she couldn't bear to think of Raif getting bad news without her. Not that she could *change* bad news, she reasoned ruefully, but she did think she could offer relief just by being there for him.

In less than thirty minutes, a knock sounded on the door and Stella departed. A maid entered with a tray of coffee and sandwiches. The food was clearly being delivered in expectation of Raif's reappearance and Claire stood up and finally allowed herself to pace.

There was no fanfare to Raif's return. The door opened quietly and he walked in equally quietly, his lean, strong face as stiff and furiously composed as it had been when he'd left her.

'Was it bad news?' she whispered, still crazily hoping that there had been some kind of melodrama that had got everybody hot and bothered by something that was in reality not as important as it initially seemed.

Raif glanced in her direction, but it was almost as if he didn't really see her well enough to focus on her. She realised then that he was suffering from shock.

'The very worst,' he told her flatly.

'Come and sit down,' Claire urged, tugging his sleeve.

'I can't. The jet's on standby at the airport. I have to fly out to Quristan immediately for...f-for,' he stammered, 'the funerals.'

'You can still have a hot drink and a sandwich before you leave,' she told him firmly.

Like a robot, he dropped down into the armchair closest to him. 'My brothers were travelling through the mountains. As my father's heirs, they are not supposed to travel in the same vehicle, but Kashif tells me that they routinely ignored his edict. There was an avalanche. The car and the security car behind it went off the road into a ravine. Hashir and Waleed, their driver and bodyguards are all dead,' he told her in the same measured tone.

Claire dropped onto her knees by his side and reached for his hand. 'I'm so very sorry,' she muttered, fighting back tears, for even she had not imagined such a terrible tragedy.

Raif squeezed her hand and instantly withdrew his own. His dark eyes shone with tears. 'I never really knew them. Over the years when I visited, I always told myself that there was time to get to know them, but now that future possibility has gone with them.' Swallowing convulsively, Claire bowed her brow against his knee because she knew what those feelings could do to a person. All the years that she was growing up she had made herself believe that once she was an adult, she would manage to build a better relationship with her father, that he would like her more and understand her better once she was mature and settled into her career. Only she hadn't got the chance either when her father had passed away quite suddenly. Disappointed hopes, things done and said or not done and said, all of it piled high on top of grief. Yes, she knew exactly what Raif was feeling and struggling to contain. And the worst fact of all in such situations was that there were rarely good memories to revisit as a consolation.

'I must leave,' Raif breathed abruptly, pushing himself upright again with force. 'My father is in Intensive Care. He had a heart attack when he was told about the death of my brothers. I need to see him.'

'Of course,' she murmured, shaken by that final, additional blow.

She wanted to ask questions, loads of questions about wives and nieces and his father's condition, but she swallowed all those enquiries back because Raif had quite enough on his plate to cope with. 'Can I come with you?'

Raif froze, stunning dark golden eyes unreadable. 'Best not. You can join me when all the formalities are complete but there would be little point in you accompanying me now.'

Two maids arrived to pack for him. His bodyguards hovered in the background. Claire approached Mohsin. 'He hasn't eaten anything. Please make sure he eats.'

'Of course, Your Royal Highness.'

It was the first time she had been addressed by that title and it hugely disconcerted her. Paling, she blinked and stepped away, returning to the bedroom to supervise the packing. In truth, her assistance was not required but it made her feel a little less surplus to requirements.

In too brief a time, Raif was gone, momentarily clasping her to him stiffly, all too aware of their audience in the embassy foyer. 'I'll phone,' he said prosaically.

'We might as well have breakfast,' Stella said brightly as Raif climbed into the waiting limo and it wended its way out of sight, demolishing, it felt like then, all Claire's hopes and dreams. The guy she had married and begun to love was gone and she had never felt more alone or abandoned in her life. 'It's almost dawn. We should eat and then go to bed for a nap.'

All of a sudden, Claire was appreciating that Raif had somehow become all the brightness in her world and that was a frightening truth for a young woman who had once cherished her independence and her strength to manage her life alone.

Stella guided her into the dining room. 'You're in shock as well,' she said gently. 'Eat and then go back to bed.'

'I'm fine. I just didn't like Raif leaving alone to deal with this,' Claire admitted stiffly.

'He wouldn't have a minute to spare you over the next few days. He'll be much too busy,' Stella explained. 'I would imagine that's why he chose not to take you with him.'

'I thought he might want to let me meet his father,' Claire whispered. 'I appreciate it wouldn't be ideal with him in a sick bed *but*—'

Stella was staring at her with a frown. 'Claire… King Jafri is unlikely to be alive this time tomorrow. It was a serious heart attack. The medics don't think he'll make it through—'

'Does Raif know that?'

Stella nodded uncomfortably. 'He should have told you.'

Claire dropped her head, the food on her plate untouched as she sipped doggedly at her tea. 'That's tragic news too,' she whispered shakily. 'He's losing everyone.'

'But not you. Try to eat. I appreciate that it's difficult in your new position, but you need to keep up your strength for the days ahead.'

What new position? Claire blinked and studied her plate, her thoughts on her baby, and she lifted the knife and fork and managed to eat a morsel of egg and toast. Her tummy felt hollow and her brain was all at sea.

'The government is afraid of instability and unrest. King Jafri was a figurehead and, although he wasn't popular, he was an institution,' Stella explained. 'Raif, however, is very popular.'

'He told me that as a third son he was very unimportant in Quristan,' Claire muttered uncomfortably.

Kashif's voice entered the conversation as he dropped down into the seat at the head of the table. 'Even at school when he was acing every exam, Raif was very modest in his attitude towards his own achievements. He's raised millions for Quristan charities. He has worked tirelessly to help the poor and disadvantaged in our country and there is no one who cares more for the place of his birth. He is very highly regarded in Quristan and he will be asked to accept the crown tomorrow.'

'The *crown*?' Claire exclaimed loudly, dragged with a vengeance from her quiet reverie of pride while she was being told that Raif was simply humble and not the wisest judge of his own status.

'Surely you were aware of that?' Stella questioned in surprise. 'It's not as if there is anyone else to take the throne.'

'Didn't his brothers have children, who come first?' Claire almost whispered in her shock at what she was being told.

'Hashir had girls and Waleed had no kids. The line of succession to the throne is determined by the male collateral line,' Kashif informed her.

'I had no idea,' she admitted.

'There is no one else now,' Stella informed her quietly. 'Raif will be King and you will be Queen. Neither of you has a choice.'

'Raif would never turn his back on his duty,' Kashif interposed gently, scanning Claire's ghostly pale face and arrested expression. 'He will need you ten times more tomorrow than he needed you today.'

'Excuse me...' Claire could feel that single morsel of toast rising back as nausea threatened to overcome her and she scrambled in haste from the chair and fled back upstairs to the privacy of the bathroom.

Afterwards, she looked at her wan, perspiring face in the mirror. No potential queen could ever have looked rougher, she reflected sickly. A king and a queen? It was as if the world around her had gone insane. Claire was overwhelmed with panic and the sheer impossibility of her ever being able to live up to such a role...or Raif even thinking for one moment that she was good enough for the challenge. My goodness, had ever a guy had *greater* cause to regret his hasty marriage?

CHAPTER SEVEN

CLAIRE ENDEAVOURED TO relax on the sundeck of the *Mahnoor*, only that was impossible with her audience.

It was no longer possible for her to be alone, it seemed. Government-appointed bodyguards had arrived to team up with the security squad Raif had already cursed her with. Her apparent rise in status, announced only by the sound of the crew referring copiously to her as 'Your Majesty', had been unaccompanied by any warning or, indeed, explanation from her married-in-haste husband, the new *King* of Quristan.

It had been announced on the television news, as well as the speculation that the new Queen was of British extraction, so on that basis she assumed it was true and she had been miraculously promoted to being royal even though she knew that she was manifestly unsuitable for such a role. She was an assistant chef, for goodness' sake, only accidentally lifted to the lofty heights of royalty by the conception of their son!

When Claire had left the embassy in Barcelona, having been informed that the *Mahnoor* was in port awaiting her arrival, the quay had been packed with paparazzi, shouting questions and waving cameras but she had been swept on board by her team with all the smooth inaccessibility required by a celebrity accustomed to such limelight and avoiding it. Unfortunately, that level of public attention was so great a shock to Claire's system that it utterly unnerved her.

The first morning, Gregoire had arrived to personally give her a breakfast of eggs Benedict in her bed because he knew it was her favourite treat. That had been a sufficient surprise, particularly when he'd beamed at her and offered his congratulations on her marriage. Captain Hastings had followed later that day, proffering the good wishes of the whole crew for her future happiness. In fact, onboard the yacht, everyone seemed totally happy for her and Raif, not even hint-ing that she was as unbefitting as she knew herself to be, and that had amazed her.

Raif, however, had neglected to surprise her, finally getting in touch two long days after the event to inform her that his father had died, having only briefly regained consciousness during his vigil by the older man's bedside.

'And now you're a king!' she had pointed out almost aggressively.

And Raif had hummed and hahed, as if that small fact weren't of any real importance in the current state of chaos, and he had dared to ask her instead and repeatedly how *she* was! He had buried three of his estranged family members in succession and gained a crown and, incredibly, he was acting as though it were just another day at the office!

'I *can't* be a queen!' she had warned him straight away. 'I'm just not cut out for that sort of thing.'

'Neither am I,' Raif had countered levelly. 'But sometimes we have to do what we have to do and take the rough with the smooth.'

He was good at platitudes, not so good at dealing with the crux of an issue, she acknowledged unhappily. He hadn't taken her response seriously because, typically hugging his personal feelings to himself, he was busy acting as if everything were absolutely normal. How was she supposed to deal with that? How was any ordinary woman supposed to respond to being raised without warning to such elevated status in a country she had never even visited? And how could she baldly admit that she didn't want any of it?

Was he even considering those facts? That she didn't speak the language or know the culture or the history or even the smallest thing useful for such a position? She had tried to get those points across but he hadn't been listening. Indeed, in Claire's opinion, he had stubbornly *refused* to listen to her perfectly valid points. And he had completed that piece of male idiocy by simply telling her that she would be picked up by helicopter the next morning before the yacht sailed into British waters.

It was not that Raif was dense about everything like other men she had met, Claire conceded, feeling guilty over her critical thoughts. When she had returned to the yacht to occupy the giant stateroom that was Raif's she had found it complete with the biggest cat tree and most luxurious cubby cat bed in existence.

Circe, now restored to her mistress, was living life to the manner born. She was back to roaming the boat with her cast, restrictive head collar and a forlorn look of cat martyrdom that ensured she received loads of sympathetic attention and every treat available. And at night, her pet curled up in a cosy bed lined with fur. So, Raif had thought about her cat's needs in spite of his family losses and sudden gaining of a throne and it was just a shame that he preferred not to address his wife's feelings or needs about those same developments.

Raif sprang out of the helicopter and strode for his bride's hiding place, apparently the rarely used private sun deck attached to their stateroom. He knew that courtesy of Mohsin, who at his instigation had remained in Spain to watch over Claire. He reckoned that even the bodyguard had registered that Claire was freaking out at the prospect of what lay ahead of her because she had not left the owner's suite since she had boarded.

Raif had been surrounded on all sides by people advising him that he shouldn't leave the country again so soon after arriving and certainly not while still in official mourning. He had defied all that unwelcome advice. He was too well aware of what he had to do to even listen to their strictures. He was not his father, chary of foreign travel and change of all kinds. He was not afraid to be different and he could not afford to be. He was willing to sacrifice a lot to be the monarch Quristan required but he was *not* willing to risk losing his wife.

Claire was in the stateroom staring at all the suitcases that had been packed for her while she was out on deck with her book. What a coward she was, she thought painfully. She had not flat out told Raif that she *wasn't* planning to fly out to Quristan. She had texted him and merely said that she wasn't ready to travel…*yet* being the optimum word included because she didn't have the guts to tell him that their imprudent marriage was surely over and that he should get a divorce in the pipeline as soon as possible.

After all, in such circumstances, what else could they do? Neither one of them had even considered that such tragedies could occur and radically change the whole landscape of their lives.

She moved out to the sun deck to return to the book she was reading. It had been a relief to discover that most of Raif's books were in English. She had been reading about the history of Quristan, which seemed to her to relate to constant fierce fights between varying tribes right up until his father had assumed the throne. Since those long-ago days, however, democracy had arrived and peace and prosperity had settled in for most of the kingdom.

'Claire…?'

She spun round in disbelief when she heard Raif's familiar drawl. And there he stood, sheathed in a tailored suit as was his wont and indisputably looking totally, utterly breathtaking in his gorgeousness. Olive skin, cropped black hair, stunning bone structure…not to mention his lithe and muscular physique. Dazzling dark golden eyes held hers fast for several seconds and she was literally pinned to the spot. Her heartbeat sped up, her nipples tightening into taut buds, her complexion flushed as she approached the patio doors where he stood. 'We need to talk,' she semi-whispered, woefully aware of all the listening ears around them.

'Yes,' Raif agreed in the mildest of tones as he guided her indoors again where at least they would have privacy.

He rammed the sliding door back into place and turned. Lean, strong face bland, he reacted to the knock on the stateroom door by crossing the room to answer it. A crewman entered with a luggage trolley and began to pile on her cases. Claire froze, bit her lower lip and waited until the trolley had exited again before murmuring flatly, 'I wasn't expecting you to make a personal visit.'

'I would guess not,' Raif conceded with the shadowy edge of an unexpectedly sardonic smile that tugged at the corners of his compressed lips.

'But it won't change anything,' she declared baldly, mustering her arguments while refusing to look at him any longer. 'I'm not returning to Quristan with you. I'm planning to return to London and let you get on with a divorce. As short-lived as our marriage has been, I shouldn't think it would take long to wipe it out again. We could even lie and say the marriage wasn't consummated and have it dissolved.'

Raif marvelled at her naivety, considering that she was pregnant with *his* child. But he was simultaneously appalled by how much her outlook had changed in the space of a handful of days. In little more than a week and a half, he had been condemned and found wanting by a woman who didn't think enough of herself to even contemplate that she could be his queen. That in itself was the bigger sin, but, as he recognised the same weakness in himself, he was unwilling to allow it to destroy their future. He could only see his future as being with her, the two of them *together*. They were a couple, stronger with each other than without, and as a family they would face and handle any and all difficulties that might threaten them.

'You're full of inventive ideas,' he remarked.

Claire stiffened, braced her hands on her hips in what she hoped was a pose guaranteed to emphasise her strength of purpose. 'Let's face it... I'm not queen material.'

'It's a personal opinion, of course,' Raif breathed, studying the picture she made in a flowing turquoise sundress that highlighted her anxious blue eyes, guiltily conscious of the all too ready quickening at his groin and the incipient throb of arousal. 'But I believe you'll make an amazing queen. You're down to earth, practical and normally steady under stress. Everything that makes you efficient in catering will make you perfect to stand by my side.'

Her troubled eyes opened very wide. 'That's ridiculous, Raif,' she told him with deep conviction. 'Queens are all about women who wear silk and fabulous tiaras! Have you looked at your late mother's jewellery?'

Hearing the edge of panic in her voice, Raif merely laughed with genuine appreciation. 'Claire, my mother was Queen in another era, for a generation long buried. Luckily, the world has changed and moved on. You are a working woman with a career and that is much more relatable to our people. A social butterfly like my mother, only seen on ceremonial occasions wearing that fabulous jewellery, would be much less admired and desirable these days.'

'I disagree,' Claire declared firmly as he strode past her to let Circe enter through the sun-deck glass door and join them. *Her* pet that proceeded to fawn at *his* feet in the most embarrassing way.

'Circe was born to be a royal cat,' Raif pointed out cheerfully. 'She just knows she's a queen and dares us all to treat her any other way. Our leading newspaper has asked permission to develop a cartoon around her. I suspect that Circe has the chops to become much more famous than either of us.'

'A *cartoon*?' Claire gasped incredulously. 'But how does anyone even *know* that I own a cat?'

'You can blame me for that. I have provided certain facts about you, that you're an English chef and you have a cat,' he admitted levelly. 'I'm very proud of my wife. She's strong and beautiful and she has her feet on the ground like a contemporary queen should have.'

Losing colour at those disconcerting assurances, Claire became very tense, the weight of his expectations bearing down on her and feeling like a judgement rather than a vote of confidence. 'Look, we're not going to agree about this. You think I can do it. I know I *can't*. There's no room for a compromise there.'

Another knock sounded on the door. On the way to answer it, Raif scooped up Circe and went out into the corridor with her. A dim exchange of voices was heard. Claire frowned but stayed where she was until he reappeared. 'What have you done with my cat?'

'Oh, she's all set for the palace. Has no doubts whatsoever regarding her future,' Raif told her airily. 'So, this is as close as I will ever come to blackmail. The cat's coming to Quristan. Will you come too?'

'For goodness' sake!' Claire spluttered, torn between anger and amusement at that move. 'Raif...'

'Are you really prepared to give up what we have together?'

Claire got flustered. 'It's not fair to ask me that. These are very, very unusual circumstances. We got married and it was ordinary—'

'And now we have the opportunity to

make our marriage *extraordinary*,' Raif sliced in with fierce determination. 'You're prepared to give up without even trying to make it work with me?'

'Stop making it all sound like it's simple!' Claire wailed accusingly. 'You were like that on the phone when you called…acting like everything was still the same.'

'Between you and me, it *should* be the same,' Raif stated with uncompromising confidence. 'Nothing else should matter but you and me and our son. Nothing should come between us.'

'I *can't* do it!' she exclaimed in a pained rush.

'But giving up without even giving it a go is cowardice.'

'That's a low blow.'

'But it's the truth. If I let you go, will you look back on this decision as something you're proud of…or will you always wonder what might have been?'

Tears stung her eyes like mad. She was furious with him. He had confronted her with so many unanswerable questions. He had warned her that fear of the unknown shouldn't be allowed to influence such a major decision. Unmistakeably, he was telling her the truth and how could she fault a man for telling her the truth, no matter how little she wished to hear it?

'Claire, be reasonable,' he murmured levelly. 'You're my wife. You're carrying my son. I value what we have. I want you to remain a part of my life.'

'Shut up!' she condemned on the back of a sob, no longer convinced that she could take the path she had planned. When push came to shove, actually walking away from Raif felt comparable to sticking a knife in her own chest and she had never been of a self-destructive bent.

'I need you to keep me level,' Raif breathed in a raw undertone. 'Absolutely nobody will tell me to shut up now.'

'I just can't do it!' she exclaimed, stricken, tears choking her. 'I'm not good enough or clever enough to be a queen...even for you!'

'I understand,' Raif murmured flatly, walking back to the door, propping it open with the holder. 'I *do* understand but I can't let you make this decision for us both.'

'What does that mean?' Claire whispered tearfully.

'That sometimes fate needs a bloody good push!' Raif intoned as he swung her up into his arms and locked her in place over one powerful shoulder.

'What on earth are you doing?'

'I believe I'm abducting you. I'd be grateful if you didn't scream, but even if you scream blue murder I'm *still* abducting you.'

Two small fists struck his back in concert. 'You have to be joking!' she launched back as he strode out into the corridor and straight up the steps to the top deck and the helipad.

'I never joke about serious stuff...and this *is* serious,' Raif pointed out almost conversationally.

'Raif...put me down! You *can't* do this!'

'International waters? King? I think I'll get away with it,' Raif quipped as he strode to the helipad and very carefully lifted her again to stow her into the helicopter as if she were made of impossibly delicate glass that might shatter.

Since there was absolutely no point in trying to argue above the noise of the helicopter, Claire donned her protective headphones, gritted her teeth and stared into the distance until it was time to get out at the airport. On arrival, they immediately crossed the tarmac to board the private jet awaiting them and she didn't fancy throwing a scene in front of the assembled air crew stationed at the foot of the boarding steps. Flanked by bodyguards, they boarded the jet.

Facial muscles tight as highly strung wires, Claire dropped straight down into an opulently upholstered tan leather seat and buckled in, her temper like a sharpened razor because Raif had no right, no right whatsoever, to force her into doing what she did not want to do. And she didn't care whether or not that was craven, *did she*? Her husband had kidnapped her to make her do his bidding and that was unpardonable. She simmered like a pot of oil over a fire as the bodyguards left the main cabin to settle into the rear one and the jet prepared for take-off.

'Claire…?'

'I'm not speaking to you,' she told him, even though she knew that she was too mad to keep her feelings locked up tight and would inevitably speak to him.

'This way, we get a chance to see if we can still work,' Raif breathed tautly. 'Your way? We would have no chance at all. I couldn't accept that.'

'*My* way had advantages. I could have slipped off the stage of your new life as if I'd never been there in the first place,' Claire protested vehemently. 'If you have not been seen in public with me it could have been done *quietly* and the divorce could surely have been achieved discreetly as well.'

'How quiet and discreet do you expect me to be while you steal my son from me?'

Claire's mouth fell open in shock at that response. *'Steal?'*

'What else do you call it? You leave and my son goes with you?'

'For goodness' sake, he's not even born yet!' Claire proclaimed, ramming loose her seat belt to stand up now that the jet was airborne.

Raif subjected her to a fulminating appraisal. 'Yes, I would in all probability miss out on his birth as well, as divorced couples are unlikely to share such an event. I would also miss out on a great deal more. I will not be free to travel whenever I like and, since I assume you would plan to base yourself in the UK, I could at best hope to be only an occasional caller in my son's life. That is unacceptable to me.'

Claire was outraged by his raising of perfectly valid points that she had not considered. Maybe it was a sign of her lack of future vision, she thought furiously, but her infant son was only a passenger in her life at present and she was not already thinking of his birth and his life beyond that. 'You're not being reasonable!' she condemned, already terribly afraid that *she* was the one being unreasonable.

'You're only just realising that after I abducted you?' Raif came back at her drily as he too rose to his feet. 'I will not be reasonable, as you call it, when you're threatening to deprive our son of a father. I *had* no father! He was a man in the distance in a crowd and we never got any closer than that. That was the result of a divorce. Divorce can only be a bad word in my vocabulary!'

Claire was thoroughly disconcerted by the anger Raif was no longer striving to hide. His caramel-gold eyes were bright with annoyance, his lean, strong face set into hard lines. Suddenly she was being bombarded by undeniable facts.

'I felt it was too soon to be thinking of our child,' she muttered unevenly. 'I'm sorry about that. I should have considered the effect of a divorce on your access to him.'

'You should also keep in your mind,' Raif murmured dulcetly, 'that that little boy will be Crown Prince of Quristan from the moment he is born. That is his birthright, his heritage, and his path now.'

Claire lost colour and sank back heavily into her seat because once again that was a reality that had not entered her head and she was deeply embarrassed by her failure to identify that fact.

Raif sat back down again as well. 'Being in the palace now is a *very* steep learning curve for me, Claire, because I didn't grow up there and I wasn't trained for my role. There are strange traditions to be respected, ceremonies that I am unversed in. Growing up in the UK deprived me of more than I appreciated at the time. My summers with my great-uncle in the desert were not quite as educational as I once naively assumed,' he concluded grimly.

As the awful silence fell, smouldering with unhappy, dissatisfied undertones,

Claire was cut to the bone with mortification. She swallowed hard. How could she not have thought of their child's needs or their child's future in Quristan? And yet she hadn't, probably because all that seemed too distant while also being utterly unfamiliar to her. She was someone who took a broad view of events, not a detached, detailed view. But she was very much shaken by Raif's bitter admission that even as the King he was struggling to find his path at the palace because he had not been raised with that background. He was working to fit in. She recognised that trait in him: if he failed at something, he would probably just work harder and he would blame himself for any mistakes or omissions.

And where did such a sterling character trait leave her in comparison? She had been ready to run in fear and panic, ready to turn her back on the new and unfamiliar without even taking account of her son's needs or giving their new life a chance. She hadn't thought that far ahead, she excused herself unhappily. But the lowering truth was that Raif *was* thinking that far ahead and already foreseeing the pitfalls of a divorce because he had grown up with separated parents and a father he had never got to know.

Raif glanced at her, his amazing black-lashed tortoiseshell eyes calm again. 'I haven't been fair to you, but I couldn't let you and our child leave me like that.'

Moisture was prickling at the backs of her eyes and she nodded stiffly. 'I hadn't thought everything through. I was panick-ing.'

'I know. I too am still finding my way in this role, and I will be for some time,' he admitted in a harsh undertone. 'But people are depending on me to succeed, and I will do the best I can.'

All of a sudden, she wanted to grab his hand, do something physical to show him that she truly understood, but she couldn't reach him where he sat on the other side of the aisle and clasped her hands together tightly instead. 'I'll give it a go,' she prom-ised abruptly. 'But my best... I warn you... may not be good enough.'

'I only ask that you *try*. Give us some time in which to adapt to these changes,' he urged.

'I'm sorry you had to abduct me,' she told

him in all seriousness. 'But in a way, I sort of enjoyed it too…'

Raif gazed back at her in wonderment and then he threw back his head and laughed with huge appreciation. 'This is why I wanted you back, Claire. I haven't laughed once since I last saw you.'

'You haven't had anything to laugh about.' She sighed.

Raif studied her from below drowsy lashes. He was so tired. Indeed, he had never been more tired in his life. The funerals, his father's passing as well as certain painful facts he had learned in recent days, not to mention the demands on his time and understanding, had all combined to plunge him into exhaustion. The prospect of Claire leaving his life, however, had galvanised him into a level of aggressive action he could barely credit in the aftermath. But now she was here with him. Claire *and* his child. Relief was slowly filtering through him, pushing out the tension that had filled him with stolen energy. His sensible queen…his sensible, sexy queen… A dim smile formed on his expressive lips before he fell asleep.

The door at the far end of the cabin opened

a crack and Circe prowled into view, set free from her carrier. Claire lifted her pet onto her lap and stroked her. Tea was brought and sandwiches and a bunch of fashion magazines she had not the faintest interest in when she was about to start searching out maternity wear. She watched Raif sleep, his bronzed features smoothed out by rest, making him look younger. But he would rise to the challenges ahead of him…and now she was committed to rising to those same challenges because she loved him to bits. How could she ever have convinced herself that she would be able to walk away from him?

CHAPTER EIGHT

THEY ARRIVED IN Quristan without fanfare.

Kazan, the capital city, also had the main airport. Within minutes they were tucked into an SUV with dark windows and, with a cavalcade of security in attendance, driven through the city. It was a much more urban contemporary landscape than Claire had naively expected, for the skies were full of towering skyscrapers, including several obvious city landmarks, which were of architectural significance.

'My father hated all this development but there wasn't anything he could do about it,' Raif told her wryly. 'We were not greeted by journalists when we landed because early in his reign my father imposed draconian rules on the media.'

'Why?'

Raif grimaced. 'When he was a young

man in Spain, there was that scandal with the young woman, and he blamed the media for it. He was very shaken up and determined to ensure that such a thing never happened to him or the family again. It made him very controlling in his behaviour. Now, of course, the government wants the media restraints loosened. In fact, the government pretty much wants to roll back everything my father supported to prevent Quristan from joining the rest of the modern world. But they will have to do it slowly to keep the traditionalists happy.'

'And where do you stand?' Claire asked, turning back from an appreciative scrutiny of a gleaming shopping mall and the cleanliness of the street.

'In the middle ground. I'm fresh to all this and I have to learn and listen more than direct, which is hard. I've been my own boss for too long,' he reflected. 'But I can utilise my experience in business and development, which is good.'

The palace was a vast hotchpotch of stone buildings set in the desert beyond the city. Surrounded by tall stone walls, it resembled a fortress more than a palace until the SUV pulled through the gates and she glimpsed the greenery, fountains and shaded pathways within the enclosure.

'It looks medieval.'

'It is at its core but since the onslaught of my father's second wife it rejoices in every modern comfort on the market. It's more like a hotel than a home. The staff quarters, however, are shockingly poor and the kitchens are hundreds of years behind the times. You are free to make improvements.'

'Me?' she exclaimed in surprise.

'You must certainly know how to modernise a kitchen and utilise health and safety rules to make improvements. As for our future home, you may consult with the builders I've brought in.'

'I thought this was our future home?'

'My father's private quarters belong in a museum.'

'With the Count Dracula bed?' she asked with a wince of dismay.

Raif nodded confirmation. 'Every room in his wing is like that. Very ornate, grand and dark. He didn't allow my mother's replacement wife to change anything there. It's not where I want to spend my down time, and

190 THE BABY THE DESERT KING MUST CLAIM

eventually I would like to open that part of the palace to the public, so it must be left as it is.'

'Then where do we live?'

'In the old section of the palace. It's a massive building. Every generation extended it,' he explained, handing her out of the vehicle with care. 'Our staff are waiting inside to welcome us.'

A huge throng of people awaited them indoors. And indoors was totally unexpected. The foyer rejoiced in all the opulence of an exclusive hotel, which Raif had mentioned, and he had hit that luxurious but soulless note right on target in his description. There was no character, nothing to ground the reality that it was the royal palace of Quristan. Claire moved forward to accept introductions but there so many faces and so many job titles, she knew she would have to learn them at a slower pace. Shahbaz, the head of household, she would remember for his carefully coiffed grey hair and moustache, but other faces were not so easy to commit to memory.

'Now come and meet my uncle, Prince

Umar. He's my mother's little brother,' Raif informed her fondly.

He was a small, rotund man with white hair and a white beard and, with a twinkle in his kind dark eyes as he greeted her, he bore a striking resemblance to Santa Claus. He turned his head to call someone and a slender brunette in a black dress stepped forward with a rather anxious smile as though she were intimidated either by her surroundings or the company.

'Your Majesty,' she said breathlessly, bowing her head to Raif.

For a split second, Raif seemed frozen in place by surprise and then a stiff smile slowly crossed his face. 'Nahla, how are you?' he said, before turning to Claire to say, 'This is Nahla, my uncle's ward.'

'Nahla needs occupation,' his uncle announced cheerfully. 'And I thought work at the palace would be perfect for her now that she and the girls are living with me.'

'You're living with my uncle again?' Raif queried with a frown.

'Since my husband died, yes,' Nahla said uncomfortably. 'I'm sorry, I thought you would have heard but then how would you have? It's been some time since your last real visit.'

'Nahla, go and chat to my wife,' Umar instructed. 'I'll explain in private, Raif.'

Raif moved on to greet someone else, a light hand at Claire's spine carrying her along. 'What's the secrecy about?' she whispered.

'I don't know,' he said in a curiously flat voice. 'I've known Nahla since I was a teenager. My uncle and aunt had only one child, a daughter. She died tragically young and when Nahla was orphaned, they took her in because she was their daughter's best friend. She married straight out of school to a much older man. I didn't realise he'd died.'

'And she has children?'

'Two or three. I'm not quite sure how many,' Raif admitted wryly. 'They'd be at school by now, I would think.'

As Raif was cornered by an older man with an air of importance, his uncle appeared at Claire's elbow. 'I was hoping that Nahla might find favour with *you*,' he stressed in a hopeful undertone. 'She could be a big help to you here. She speaks your language and would be a good guide.'

'Of course,' Claire agreed, not really knowing what else to say, but it scarcely needed to be said that Claire was an uninformed complete beginner in the royal family. She would need advice on who was who and how to behave and all sorts of things. In fact, her head just spun at the prospect of all that she had still to learn about Quristan, the Quristani people and her new role.

'Thank you,' he said, as though she had given him a promise when she had not.

Raif returned to her side to usher her into a lift concealed by fancy panelling. 'Let me show you where we will be living for the present.'

'You mean, there's going to be more than one move?'

Raif dealt her an apologetic appraisal. 'Possibly. It depends how much you like the building that I've chosen and if you can tolerate living in the middle of a construction site.'

Claire laughed. 'Will it be that bad?'

They emerged from the lift into a huge airy space. 'This is the entrance hall, and we will have three floors of rooms,' he explained with enthusiasm. 'You will be relieved to hear that the bathrooms have already been installed.'

Claire nodded slowly and almost laughed again. Yes, she would have been loud in her complaints without those facilities. It occurred to her that engaging in the renovation of their living quarters had inspired Raif with a lighter mood than she had seen him show since the combined tragedy that had deprived him of his brothers and his father. Of course, design and development were crucial elements of his property empire, she reminded herself, so it was hardly surprising that he should relax within a familiar field.

She remained mostly silent while he showed her round incredibly grand large rooms being stripped down to their antique bones to preserve the character. In every room, workmen downed tools and bowed with extreme formality. Raif, evidently, had a vision, but when he stopped in the most massive space she had ever seen in a property and told her that it would be their bedroom her eyes widened. 'Why so big?'

'Because we're sharing it.'

'Well, of course, we're going to share,' she muttered.

'But that's not the norm in the palace,' Raif explained with his sudden flashing smile. 'According to Shahbaz, no previous ruler has shared a bedroom with his spouse. Partly because you will need a maid to look after your wardrobe and I will need a valet and that entails separate dressing areas, therefore we shall need a very big space to cover those necessities.'

Claire couldn't imagine having a maid merely to preside over her clothes and she simply nodded as though she understood, because she could not even imagine Raif sleeping in another bedroom, or, at least, she didn't want to even picture such an arrangement and the loss of intimacy that would result. She suspected that their bedroom would be the only place where they got to be genuinely alone, which was rather an intimidating acknowledgement. He showed her into the bedroom that he was currently occupying and her heart, which had been sinking on that last thought, lifted at a glimpse of familiar items.

As she paused to absently stroke the back

of a carved wooden brush on a dresser, Raif's phone buzzed and he checked it with a frown.

'I must return to the ground floor,' he said simply. 'There are people awaiting my reappearance. I should make the effort to speak to them.'

Claire connected with his brilliant dark golden eyes and a tingle ran over her entire skin surface. That was the effect Raif always had on her. Sometimes it felt like touching a live wire, an electric surge of energy that flared through her whole body, awakening every intimate nerve cell. Her breasts felt full, the core of her pulsing, sending colour to flare over her cheekbones.

Raif studied her with flaring intensity and paced forward. 'I do not want to leave you here alone.'

'I will be fine,' Claire told him more calmly than she felt, reckoning that their future would be full of such moments. He would always be carrying the burden of large expectations. She was an adjunct as his queen, not a leading light. She couldn't step in for him, she could only offer the support of understanding.

'I'll order tea for you,' he told her. 'The room next door is a sitting room and furnished…' A groan escaped him and he drove his fingers through his thick black hair in a gesture of frustration and embarrassment. 'That I should tell you that it is *furnished* as though that were some kind of consolation.'

'Raif…' Claire lifted her hand and stretched up to tidy his hair again. 'Stop worrying about me. I'm good at managing and at being independent.'

'Yes, *but*—'

'No buts,' she declared cheerfully. 'You didn't marry a woman who needs you hovering over her every minute of the day. I'm not helpless.'

And then he was gone, and she swallowed back the thickness in her throat and walked to the room next door. A few minutes later an older woman arrived with a tray, and she was in the act of pouring a cup of tea when a knock sounded on the ajar door.

'Yes?' she called.

Nahla appeared on the threshold. 'I'm so sorry to disturb you, Your Majesty,' she murmured tautly. 'But I wanted to apologise for my uncle's behaviour.'

'Please come in and sit down,' Claire suggested, seeing the brightness of tears in the delicate brunette's eyes and marvelling that she could look so sad without losing an atom of her soulful beauty. 'Prince Umar didn't say anything which could have caused offence,' she declared calmly.

Nahla sat down awkwardly opposite. 'But he is downstairs now cornering your husband. He will list my recent…er misfortunes and attempt to push Raif into hiring me onto the household staff. It is very trying, and I can assure you that I am *not* expecting you to employ me. I have no special skills to offer. I have only been a wife and a mother since I left school. I know little about the world beyond our borders. But now I'm a widow, even worse, the widow of a bankrupt, and those facts are a social embarrassment to my uncle and aunt.'

'And you and your children live with them,' Claire recalled quietly. 'That must be awkward.'

Nahla flushed. 'They have been very good to me. Please believe that I am not complaining. But my uncle can be too insistent in his requests without meaning to be and once he gets an idea in his head, he is very stubborn.'

Claire offered her tea and let her talk, recognising that she was distressed. Nahla had gone through depression and a nervous breakdown after losing the husband she described as her soulmate and the loss of the business that had supported her family had been an additional blow.

'You speak terrific English,' Claire remarked.

Nahla smiled. 'I attended an English school up until my parents died.'

'And you speak the language here and know the culture and presumably many of Quristan's VIPs,' Claire commented as Nahla nodded in understated confirmation. 'Well, then, I would like to offer you a job. I need someone to interpret Quristani life for me. Raif will be too busy to help me much.'

It took quite a bit of convincing for Nahla to be persuaded that she could be of help. The other woman had a low estimate of her own abilities and clearly felt both uneducated and insufficiently well-travelled to suit such a role. But Claire had taken a liking to her and knew that she would much prefer someone sincere and unassuming like Nahla to some polished court official who might well make *her* feel inadequate.

An hour later as Raif returned to his private wing of the palace he was inwardly celebrating the fact that he had successfully and with great tact derailed his uncle's hope of palming Nahla off on the royal household. The very last thing he needed was daily exposure to the woman he had fallen in love with as a teenager, and it would be horribly inappropriate for her to work for his wife. His loyalties had changed, he recognised with wry acceptance. Once he would have done anything to aid Nahla, and, indeed, she had his full sympathies in her current plight. However, Claire was his wife and the future mother of his son and his strongest loyalty now belonged to her...

CHAPTER NINE

CLAIRE WAS FEELING mightily pleased with herself by the time evening fell. She had been very busy, and she loved being busy.

She had got on with Nahla like a house on fire. Only Nahla would have stepped straight into the job of acting as Claire's guide and interpreter the same day that she accepted the position. Claire had fully explored the section of the palace that was to be their home and decided where she wanted certain things and, there being no shortage of either rooms or space, it had been a most enjoyable enterprise. Of course, over dinner she would have to run her ideas past Raif first and gauge his reaction.

After reaching those decisions, she had asked Nahla to escort her down to the palace kitchen and conditions down there in the string of basement rooms that acted as the palace kitchens had horrified her. Shahbaz, the head of household, had joined them and waxed lyrical in his agreement that something had to be done to renovate those dark medieval caves.

Nahla had contrived to find them a table and chairs for a room that could act as a dining room for her and Raif in the short term. Thanks to Nahla's presence, she had even been able to tell the chef in the basement what sort of food Raif liked to eat. Who knew better than his former assistant chef on board his yacht?

Raif was emerging from the shower, wrapped in a towel, when she arrived equally bare to take advantage of the same facility. 'Thrills on top of thrills, wife,' he teased, catching her straight into his arms.

'I'm all hot and sweaty,' she lamented.

'I'm not that choosy after so many days without you,' he admitted thickly.

Claire hardened her heart against the onslaught of smouldering caramel eyes of gold. 'Well, I *am*. You have to wait for me to feel clean.'

And Raif laughed, utterly charmed by her as always. Her frank nature enchanted him. There was nothing hidden, no secret tripwires, no manipulation. Following an exhausting afternoon, delicately treading round the government officials besetting him with demands, hopes and persuasions on matters on which he needed to remain neutral, her open natural response to him was as precious as water in the desert to him.

'I will wait,' he murmured softly, nudging her hair back from her neck to plunge his long fingers into the thick golden strands and claim a single scorching kiss that lit her up in a starburst of sensation from the top of her head to the soles of her feet.

Still tingling, Claire laughed and stepped straight into the shower, happiness humming through her in a sensual wave. Forty minutes later, they sat down together at the new dining table. 'Where on earth did you get it from? I've been eating off trays and at my desk,' Raif confided.

'I couldn't have done it without Nahla, and I don't know where she got the set from. I didn't ask.' For a moment, Claire looked comically guilty. 'Oh, my goodness, I hope some other couple aren't sitting with trays now just because we get first dibs on stuff as King and Queen!'

Raif, however, didn't laugh, indeed didn't even look amused. 'Nahla?' he queried, his brows pleating in confusion. 'Nahla who?'

'You know her!' Claire quipped. 'Your uncle's ward. He was so pushy about me giving her a job.'

'I've dealt with that. You don't need to worry about hiring her,' Raif informed her stiffly. 'Umar can be too demanding.'

'Well, that doesn't matter,' Claire assured him hastily, worried that she had offended him by being too outspoken about the uncle she knew he was fond of. 'Nahla was worried that he had been rude, and she called up here to apologise and explain that she wasn't expecting to work for me.'

'That's good.' The tense set of Raif's broad shoulders relaxed a little as the first course arrived at the table and then his speech became constrained again. 'Working as your assistant would be viewed as a plum job in the palace hierarchy. It is wiser that such a position does not go to my royal uncle's ward. It could look like nepotism.'

Claire grimaced. 'Oh, dear,' she breathed in consternation. 'I hired her on the spot—'

'You did...*what*?' Raif demanded in a tone she had never heard from him before. It was both angry and disbelieving and his dark golden eyes had flared like metallic storm warnings.

'I'm sorry, Raif...if you don't approve,' Claire tacked on uncomfortably, taken aback by his annoyance. 'I should've consulted you first. I can see that now but at the time I just liked her and she does seem to be a genuinely nice person.'

Raif's lean, darkly handsome features were rigid. 'I have never heard a bad word spoken of her and she is, certainly, having a difficult time at the moment. My uncle filled me in on her late husband's bankruptcy and all the rest of it. Many of my uncle's friends lost money when the business collapsed, and it is difficult for them to have Nahla and her children in their home at present.'

'But that's not *her* fault!' Claire exclaimed.

'Of course not,' he agreed, relieving her of her fear that he had no compassion for Nahla's plight. 'And that bad feeling and embarrassment will ebb eventually, but Umar is not a patient man, and he is well aware that working at the palace would restore Nahla's reputation.'

'Will it?' Claire grinned at that assurance. 'Well, thank goodness I picked her, then. I *really* like her, Raif.'

Raif gritted his even white teeth behind a resolute smile. 'Yes, I am getting that message.'

'So, it's okay, then? Even if some people say that her getting the job is royal nepotism at work?'

'It will have to be,' Raif conceded, long brown fingers flexing round his knife and fork as he finally lifted them to begin eating. 'You can hardly go back on your word.'

'She felt like a best friend, and I miss Lottie, so it was lovely feeling as though I have a friend here where everything is different,' Claire framed in a rush.

'When we have settled in, when we no longer have to borrow or steal a dining table...' His tension ebbing because he could recognise a *fait accompli* when it happened and accept the inevitable, he continued, 'You'll be able to invite your friend, Lottie,

and her family to visit once we have a few
more rooms available for use here.'

The speed and brightness of Claire's
happy smile at that news was his reward.
Claire liked Nahla, Raif conceded ruefully.
At this point, it seemed wiser to retain his secret than to tell the unfortunate truth, bearing in mind that Claire had strictly warned
him *never* to tell her the name of the woman
he loved. And perhaps it would be good for
him, he reflected ruefully. Perhaps he could
finally put those feelings behind him where
they belonged, now that the woman he had
once obsessed over and rarely seen would
be around him occasionally. In all honesty,
he didn't *want* to tell Claire that secret, he
acknowledged, not if it might hurt or upset
her. He felt quite sick at the idea of Claire
being hurt in any way…and especially over
anything for which he was responsible.

'I explored this whole bit of the palace this
afternoon and I've had some ideas.'

Claire wanted a small kitchen installed for
her own use and Raif almost laughed when
she asked if that would be achievable. 'Anything you want is possible,' he assured her

levelly. 'This place must feel like your home as well for you to be content here.'

'And I picked a room for the baby, just across the corridor from what will ultimately be our bedroom,' she warned him. 'I'll want to choose the decoration myself.'

Raif grinned, amused that she could think such simple normal requests could be out of order. 'I want to contribute my ideas too—'

'Well, I don't want it all blue just because he's a boy. That's kind of a dated approach.'

'My father was truly full of joy when I told him we were having a boy,' Raif informed her in a tight undertone. 'In spite of all our differences, I wanted him to have that comfort and consolation in his last hours. Knowing that the succession to the throne was secured meant more to him than anything else. That was the only reason I told him that you were pregnant.'

Claire was thoroughly disconcerted by that sudden unexpected confession and she went very still, watching the unguarded emotions of regret and sorrow flit through Raif's expressive dark eyes. 'You managed to speak to him, then, *before*—'

'Yes, and I learned some things that made

me unhappy,' he admitted in a driven admission of regret. 'Hashir was forced into a divorce because of his lack of a male heir. His ex-wife and daughters had already moved out of the palace before his death. I have asked her to visit us once she is established in her new home in Kazan. I am keen to get to know my nieces.'

'What happened to Waleed's widow?' Claire asked uneasily.

'She has returned to her family as well. I gather it wasn't a very happy marriage, but in his case my father did not want them to divorce because he was still hoping Waleed might provide Hashir with a male heir,' Raif explained wryly. 'But listening to my father trying to teach me how to follow in his royal footsteps taught me a hard lesson. I assumed that my brothers had had an easier time with him than I. Now I realise that I was undoubtedly lucky to be forgotten about and freely live my life all these years without his destructive interference.'

That admission struck a familiar note in Claire's thoughts. She had learned to live with her father and stepmother's lack of attachment to her, but only now could she really comprehend what had lain behind their attitude. Her mother had inflicted a world of hurt on them both and then run away, leaving her child to ultimately reap the consequences. What Claire now knew would make it easier for her to hold out an understanding hand to her stepmother. Nothing, she had discovered, was as black and white as she had once assumed.

'My father did, however, admit that he regretted divorcing my mother and the fact that he made little effort to get to know me. He explained that he felt very guilty over causing my mother such distress and that it was easier for him just to evade any further contact with us. He then urged me to make a go of *our* marriage and not to be distracted by a pretty face when I reached middle age. I gather that, in a nutshell, is what happened to my parents' marriage. He was attracted to another woman and divorced my mother so that he could marry her,' he explained heavily. 'But that second marriage barely lasted two years before he divorced her as well.'

'Well, at least he worked out where and why he went wrong and, if he had lived longer, he probably would have tried to make amends to you,' Claire pointed out gently.

'We spoke for several hours. It was an exhausting meeting, but I do now understand my own background better.'

Before her very eyes, she was watching Raif relax and slowly shake free of the day's stress and strain. She studied him with silent, appreciative intensity, scanning his lean, sculpted bone structure, the perfect moulding of his brows and cheekbones and wide sensual mouth. Secret, delicious heat curled in her pelvis as she collided with the flare of his stunning dark golden gaze.

'I want you,' he admitted with unashamed hunger.

Claire rose from her seat, and he was just meeting her at the end of the table as the coffee arrived. He laughed and said something in his own language to Shahbaz, and linked his hand freely with hers to walk her down the corridor to their room, leaving the coffee behind untouched. Her face was red as fire.

'What must he think of us?' she muttered.

'That we are a normal couple behind the scenes,' Raif parried with quiet amusement, leaning back against the bedroom door and pulling her close to kiss her with passionate urgency. 'And this is that very special moment that I've been waiting for all day when it is finally just you and I alone together.'

Her skin tightened over her bones and warmth flooded her. Nobody had ever wanted her the way *he* wanted her, and it gave her a high that she could be that important to him. All her life she had longed to be important to someone and she had found that briefly and unforgettably with her mother, but never with anyone else she loved. That Raif, who had so many more important tasks to concentrate on, could still find time to miss her and need her, gave her a powerful sense of well-being and security.

She tipped his jacket off his shoulders and allowed it to fall. He wrenched off his tie and paused in the midst of doing so to crush her lips urgently beneath his, the flick of his tongue inside her mouth making her tremble with anticipation.

He turned her round to unzip her dress, skimmed it off her slim shoulders, pausing to run his lips across the soft smooth skin there before she stepped out of it, her knees weak, her body heating of its own accord. Lifting her onto the bed, he paused to rest his palm against the almost imperceptible but still firm swell of her no longer flat stomach. 'Our son is beginning to make his presence known,' he noted with satisfaction. 'It's incredibly sexy.'

'*Sexy?*' she repeated in astonishment. 'How can it be sexy?'

In the act of removing his shirt, Raif studied her from below his black lashes, visibly surprised by the question. 'That's our baby inside you and that can only make me feel amazingly proud.'

He spoke with such sincerity that she could not doubt him and she went from pointlessly striving to suck her tummy in to smiling and kicking off her shoes. He stripped off where he stood, unveiling lithe bronzed flesh rippling with lean muscle. For a split second he paused to take in the vision of her in her lacy, highly feminine lingerie and he marvelled that he had found her, that she asked and expected so little from him and yet freely gave him so much.

Excitement lit Claire up inside when he came down to her, fluid and graceful as a jungle cat. She loved the boneless way he moved. She loved the look of him, the scent of his skin, the very touch of him. He eased her gently free of her bra and knickers, knowing that her swollen breasts and distended nipples were tender with pregnancy. He bent his dark head and used the tip of his tongue on the sensitive peaks, until a muffled moan escaped her and her spine arched in response.

'Too much?' he asked.

Claire let her greedy fingers spear through his cropped black hair. 'Not enough,' she told him truthfully, pulling him down to her again with unhidden impatience.

Her entire being was fizzing with energy, her heart racing, her skin buzzing with the kind of need she had not even known existed until she met him. A scorching kiss sealed them close, their bodies straining into connection for the satisfaction they craved. She was ready for him, downright eager as he explored her quivering length. He grazed the tight aching buds of her nipples, delved into the tingling folds between her thighs and, that fast, that unstoppably, her body exploded into a climax. She convulsed and cried out, all tension dredged from her in a wild surge.

'And I have barely started, *aziz*,' Raif groaned.

'Is that a complaint?' she whispered shakily.

'Hell, no. Thanks to you, I'm now on an even bigger high,' he confided huskily, pressing his mouth to hers in light acknowledgement before turning her over and raising her up on her knees.

Her breath caught in her throat as he penetrated her in one fluid stroke. As her sensitive flesh stretched to accommodate him, her heart thundered and the liquid heat in her pelvis increased with an intense burst of exhilarating excitement. Every thrust of his body into hers pushed that excitement higher until she was gasping for breath, overpowered by the raw pleasure engulfing her. The muscles in her lower body pulled tighter and tighter as the tension built until his completion suddenly triggered hers. Heavens, she felt as though her body went flying off into the sun and she burned up in a wave of ecstasy, so powerful that she flopped down on the bed and promised herself that she would never willingly move again.

Raif flung himself down beside her on the tumbled sheets with an extravagant groan. 'You are amazing,' he murmured softly, trailing idle fingers through her tousled hair. 'You're very quiet. What are you thinking about?'

'What you said about seeing your father in a different light after your final meeting with him.' She sighed. 'I think it was because you're an adult now and you saw him and the past through clearer eyes. I've been going through the same process with my mother, my stepmother and my father.'

Leaning up, Raif frowned down at her. 'How?'

'Mum told me how she first met my father. She lost her parents suddenly in a car accident and she joined the church because she felt that she needed a support system. My father became that support system, advising her on everything relating to her parents' estate and, in the process, he fell in love with her,' she explained ruefully. 'But until I met Mum, I didn't know that my stepmother, Sarah, was already on the scene, a leading light in the congregation and in love with my father even then. Then Sarah had to stand by and watch him fall for my mother, which must have hurt her a great deal.'

'You're saying that your mother came between them.'

'Yes, I think he would have married Sarah if my mother hadn't appeared and that when he finally did marry her, she must have felt like second best, however untrue that was. Being forced to bring up her rival's daughter probably didn't help. And I'm not sure I've ever been fair to her. She was never unkind to me, never spiteful. She just never showed me affection the way she did with her own child.'

'You're saying she did her best but couldn't or wouldn't fake an affection she didn't feel for you. Think about something more uplifting.'

'You never ever mention your mother,' she remarked. 'Why is that?'

'I just don't like to talk about her. It feels…disloyal.' Raif turned his head away from her, his profile taut.

An awkward little silence stretched and grated on Claire's nerves, but she was hurt by his unwillingness to confide in her and it made her wonder what it was he was hiding.

'How am I going to buy maternity wear when the palace is in mourning? Shopping will be sure to be seen as frivolous at such a time.' Claire sighed, keen to change the subject to one that would hopefully remove the tension from his lean, strong face. 'And can I buy salt and vinegar crisps anywhere? If my little kitchen was up and running, I could make my own salty snacks.'

'The salespeople will come to you. I will organise it,' Raif told her soothingly. 'And Shahbaz will find you crisps.'

'I was making a mountain out of a mole-hill,' Claire gathered, and she grinned. 'I do that sometimes.'

Two and a half months later, Claire beamed at the brilliance of Raif's smile as he posed on the massive yellow excavator for the cameras aimed at him.

Ground was finally being broken at Rab-alissa, the very first step in the creation of the new port to be built on the Arabian Sea. It was a newsworthy event, and the watching crowd was filled with politicians, tribal leaders and the media. Claire was dressed for public viewing but also for practicality and cool in loose trousers and a flowing white tunic top that only hinted at the burgeoning swell of her pregnancy. Nothing dressier would have made sense when she had to trek across the equivalent of a building site.

Once the official period of mourning was over at the palace, their lives had steadily changed. Raif was now out and about most days, meeting and greeting people. Quristan was only just getting used to the idea of a young king on the throne. His father had ruled for a very long time and had only ever been seen in public on holy days and at special ceremonies. Raif was much more low-key and accessible, which went down well with the younger generation. Here in Rabalissa, the wild desolate region his mother had once ruled before her marriage to the late King, Raif was in his element overseeing the first steps in the vast development project he had instigated.

It was hot…really, *really* hot…and her tunic was sticking to her damp skin. For that reason, it was a relief when Raif returned to her side and guided her back across the rough ground into the delicious cool of the large air-conditioned temporary building where a reception was being held for the dignitaries. Raif was quickly drawn from her side to expound on the big model town set on a table in the centre of the room. Mohsin brought her ice-cold water and stuck by her side as interpreter as she made polite conversation with the people who drifted her way. Nahla was unable to travel with her because of her young children.

Raif had tried to dissuade Claire from accompanying him, but she had checked with the palace doctor that travel was fine and she had stayed by Raif's side, reluctant to let him leave her for more than forty-eight hours. It was true that the journey had been exhausting, and that she was tired and hot, but she enjoyed the rhythm of her life with Raif and knew she was likely to see a lot less of him if she used her pregnancy as an excuse and bowed out of official duties. In addition, people were as curious about her as they were about her husband, and she found it easier to be seen out and about rather than feel as if she was hiding from that interest.

At the palace, now that all the building work on their section of the palace was complete, their daily schedule had fallen into a regular pattern. First thing in the morning they shared the gym, although she was considerably less active than Raif was on the equipment. She made their lunch every day in her pristine new kitchen and, wherever Raif was and whatever he was doing, he tried to join her for that meal. Dinner, breakfast and snacks were provided by the palace chef and when she was bushed, she was grateful for the meals that arrived without any personal effort on her part. Raif agreed to only occasional evening events.

Lottie and her husband, Rob, and three children had come to stay for the weekend the month before and Claire had thoroughly enjoyed their visit, particularly when Raif had taken them all out on a sightseeing visit. Her best friend had raved about Raif and the way he treated Claire.

'He's crazy about you,' Lottie had insisted. 'He would move a mountain with his bare hands if he thought it would please you!'

And Claire had smiled politely and said nothing. No matter what Raif felt deep down inside, he would be very kind and considerate because that was the sort of man he was. He hid his innermost feelings. She might wonder how often he thought about the unavailable woman he had long loved in silence, but it was probably for the best that she had no idea. What she didn't know couldn't hurt her, she consoled herself frequently.

She had emailed her stepmother, Sarah, and invited her and her brother, Tom, out for a visit. Sarah, however, had explained that she was currently caring for her elderly mother and couldn't leave her, while Tom had a vacation job that he couldn't abandon. Her half-brother had, however, promised to fly out for a weekend during termtime. Claire had promised to call the next time she was in London, but she didn't know when that would be because the more pregnant she became, the less keen she was on travelling, particularly if it meant being without Raif.

Raif surveyed his wife from a distance and a dozen bright memories assailed him. Claire with headphones, bopping in time to music in her kitchen while she whipped up some flavoursome concoction for him to eat. Claire, remaining admirably serious when a pompous speaker at a museum event tripped over his own feet. Claire, convulsed with laughter, when he tickled her until the laughter had led into the most incredible session in their bedroom. Claire smiling, when someone enquired after Circe, the palace cat, who now rejoiced in a starring role in a newspaper cartoon. Claire chuckling at one of Mohsin's jokes, lugubrious, serious Mohsin, who had never once cracked a joke with Raif. The one talent that Claire had in spades was charm, an ability to relax people and make them feel welcome. She was so unspoilt, he sometimes marvelled that he had found a woman so perfect for him.

'Time for us to depart,' Raif whispered in her ear as he banded an arm round Claire's narrow spine. 'You're pale and you look very tired.'

'I am tired. I'm going for a nap as soon as we arrive at your mother's old home.'

'You'll like it. It's not fancy but it's comfortable. I lived there for weeks when I was working on this project. It made the perfect base.'

It was an old stone castle on a promontory high above the shoreline, overlooking the sea and a long stretch of white sand. 'Does it belong to you?' she asked as the SUV came to a halt outside the entrance.

'Technically, yes. I inherited it from my mother and she from her father, but when Rabalissa was united with Quristan, everything here supposedly went to the throne of

Quristan. My father, however, didn't use it and my mother never once visited it after their marriage. Even when she was a child, she hated the location because it was so inaccessible. That will change, of course, with the motorway that is finally being built.'

They entered the castle and moved into a hall that was filled with the cosy clutter of yesteryear, fishing rods, baskets and parasols collected in a stand, worn photos in shell frames still adorning the walls. 'Do you know who all these people are?'

'Some, but only Umar would know them all. This was his childhood home too,' he reminded her.

'Show me your mother,' she urged.

He pointed to a dark-eyed little girl in a very fussy dress.

'She was very pretty.'

'The firstborn, the future Queen of Rabalissa.' He sighed. 'Let me show you upstairs and you can lie down.'

On the wall in the graciously furnished bedroom there was a faded colour photo of a gorgeous brunette in a very glamorous outfit. 'Is that her? Your mother?' Claire asked curiously, removing her shoes and settling down on the mercifully modern divan bed awaiting her. 'She was pretty spectacular in her heyday, wasn't she?'

As Claire began to remove her clothing, Raif tensed. 'Why are you so curious about her?' he demanded.

'Because you don't talk about her,' she pointed out, folding her trousers and top. '*Why?* Of course, I wonder why. I'm only human.'

Raif strode over to the window overlooking the sea, lean back and shoulders rigid. 'Because my mother is a source of both shame and embarrassment to me,' he admitted in a terse, driven voice. 'Talking about her is difficult for me.'

As Claire dug into her suitcase for something light to wear, her brow furrowed into a frown. 'But why is that?'

'Her behaviour as my father's ex-wife in London and abroad caused many scandals and destroyed her reputation. In polite company she will not be mentioned for that reason. She became an alcoholic but also very promiscuous,' he framed curtly. 'She slept with every man available, married or otherwise. My brothers refused to be associated with her and they stopped visiting her early on. I was twelve years old when my father sent word through my siblings that I could come back to live in Quristan at the palace with him.'

Claire was very shocked by what he was finally revealing, and she quite understood his previous silence on the subject. 'My goodness,' she whispered unevenly.

'I don't think my father ever forgave me for refusing to leave her. He took that as a personal rejection but how *could* I leave her?' Raif swung back, his lean dark features pained, and he made an almost clumsy movement with his hands to accentuate the impossibility of his having made such a cruel choice. 'She only had me left. How could I abandon her as well? I was shielded from many of her affairs by boarding school. Even so, I saw much that I shouldn't have seen as an adolescent. But I loved her. I *loved* her to the bitter end when her liver failed from the alcohol.'

Claire shook her head slowly in sadness at what he had described, and her heart went out to him for the pain he was no longer attempting to conceal.

'Don't judge her from what I have told you,' Raif asked in a strained appeal. 'She was very unhappy. She had wealth and beauty but nothing she truly valued. Her depression led to her alcohol addiction and then to the men.'

'I'm so sorry, Raif,' Claire muttered heavily. 'But thank you for telling me. I think I understand you a little better now. Is that why you were still a virgin when we met?'

In silence he nodded. 'For me, sex has to be something more...*not* merely a physical thing...and the association with my mother's lifestyle repelled me.'

'I hope we're something more,' she almost whispered.

'How can you doubt it?' Raif quipped as he sank down on the bed with her and began to help her to slip out of her pretty scraps of lingerie. He dropped the nightdress over her head as though she were a child to be dressed.

He gripped her hand. 'Sleep now,' he urged. 'I'll wake you in time for dinner.'

Claire slumped into the comfortable mattress. As the door closed, she remembered what she had wanted to discuss with him and groaned. It wouldn't have been the right moment to open the topic. Raking up his mother's past had upset Raif. She would wait for a more promising opportunity to ask him if it would be possible for Nahla to move into one of the palace apartments. Raif could be rather standoffish with her assistant. Admittedly their paths rarely crossed but he had an easy manner with his own staff. With Nahla, however, he was reserved and distant. She had begun to wonder if he simply didn't like Nahla for some reason. Why didn't he just say so?

'What was he like back then?' Claire had asked Nahla fondly, some weeks earlier.

'He was quiet and serious. He always had his head in a book. He was also several years younger, so we didn't spend much time together,' Nahla had admitted, and she had giggled. 'By then, I was already falling in love with my Yousuf. I wasn't much interested in teenage boys, even though he was a royal and rather handsome prince.'

The following day, after a tour of the new resort site just along the coast and a late lunch, Claire and Raif travelled back to the palace in separate vehicles, the accident that had led to the death of both of Raif's brothers having confirmed the security risk in official circles. Until Claire had given birth to the heir to the throne, the couple had agreed to exercise caution. Unfortunately, that entailed a very long, boring and lonely drive and Claire dozed most of the way.

It was early evening when Claire reached the palace. Circe greeted her first. Shorn of her cast and her restrictive collar, the palace cat was her sleek, confident self, only now she rejoiced in a jewelled collar and a name tag, worthy of her newly acquired status as the star of a cartoon based on political satire.

The first thing Claire wanted on her return was a lengthy shower. Clad in a yellow sundress, she waited until dinner was over and they had had coffee served in the sitting room before saying, 'There's something I've been meaning to ask you, but I wasn't quite sure how to open the subject.'

'There should be nothing that you feel you cannot say to me,' Raif countered with a frown of surprise.

'Well...' Claire hesitated and sighed. 'I've noticed that you're a little uncomfortable around Nahla.'

The faintest edge of colour accentuated the slant of his hard cheekbones. 'I hardly know her,' he pointed out. 'But I have every respect for her and am grateful that you find her so useful.'

'Then, can we offer her the chance to move out of your uncle's house and move into the palace with her children?' Claire pressed in a rush.

'No,' Raif countered with finality.

Claire went pink. 'Just...*no*?'

'Yes, just no,' Raif confirmed, compressing his lips in a hard line.

'But why not?' Claire queried in bewilderment.

'The staff quarters here at the palace require renovation and until that work is complete, we can't put anyone else in substandard housing. I am, however, willing to offer her staff accommodation in Kazan, where I have bought property for that purpose,' he countered curtly. 'I would also add that I think it would be inappropriate for you to develop any closer friendship with Nahla.'

Claire reddened in surprise. 'And why would you say that? Am I suddenly supposed to turn into some sort of snob and only rub shoulders in a friendly way with VIPs?'

'Don't be ridiculous!' Raif told her curtly, pushing aside his coffee untouched and springing upright with unconcealed impatience. 'That is not what I'm saying. You must learn to respect the boundaries that we should observe. That is our life now.'

'You don't like her. That's what this is about,' Claire decided, standing up in turn, annoyed by his intransigence.

'That is untrue. I have a high opinion of Nahla…how could I not? She has been very helpful to you and she does not put herself forward.'

Claire straightened, shaken to discover that they were on the very edge of a row and wondering how that had blown up so quickly. 'Then what's your problem with her?'

Raif's brilliant dark eyes hardened. 'There is no problem.'

'Sounds like it!' Claire scoffed.

'Don't be so stubborn,' Raif urged her impatiently. 'Occasionally I will give you advice that is not to your taste and, unfortunately, this is one of those occasions.'

'That's not good enough,' Claire told him irritably. 'I want an answer. I want to know *why* you don't really like Nahla being around.'

Raif stared back at her, scanning her vivid face and the brightness of the blue eyes that had captured him at first glance. He breathed in deep and slow, wishing he could tell her the truth, wishing he could get that off his conscience but convinced that that truth would distress her and cause trouble he would struggle to handle. 'I can't tell you,' he declared with sudden harshness.

'And is this the same guy who told me that there should be nothing I can't tell *you*?' Claire responded. 'What a shame it doesn't work both ways!'

Raif swore under his breath. 'To tell you would entail breaking a promise I made you before our marriage,' he replied grimly. 'I don't know what to do for best. You tell me.'

Claire had no idea what he was referring to. She blinked, drew in a sharp breath and tried to clear her head. 'Raif…' she began quietly.

'Nahla is the woman I believed I was in love with for years,' he stated in a clipped undertone, his strain in making that admission etched in the tension clenching his lean, darkly handsome features.

CHAPTER TEN

FOR ABOUT TEN SECONDS, Claire gazed back at him, her lips parting but not a breath of sound emerging. Shock was flooding her in a tidal wave. She went white. She felt sick. She also felt unbelievably stupid.

How on earth had she been so blind? How on earth had she forgotten that promise she had asked for prior to their marriage? She had warned him never ever to tell her the identity of the woman he loved and, being Raif, he had tried to stick to that agreement until she made it impossible for him by continuing to demand answers. Without another word, she left the room, her steps merely quickening when Raif called her name after her to try and halt her flight.

She raced down the stairs into the hall. And where was she going to run? And what would running avail her? There was no running away, no escaping such an unlovely truth. Once that confession was out, there was no avoiding it, no denying it either. But what could she possibly have said to him in response to that explanation?

She had brought Nahla into Raif's radius again. *She* had fought to employ Nahla, whom she had taken an immediate liking to, a liking that had not wavered once in the weeks since she had met the other woman. Nahla was quiet, discreet, efficient and obliging. She was also strikingly beautiful in that ethereal, delicate, soulful-eyed way. Raif had attempted to dissuade her from hiring Nahla and she had ignored him, much as she had ignored his unease around the other woman, she recalled sickly. It had never occurred to her to suspect that something truly important lay behind his reluctance to employ Nahla.

From the hall, she went out through the French windows into their private courtyard. Stately palm trees of several varieties made it a highly ornamental space surrounding a beautiful mosaic-tiled fountain where water fanned down softly into a pond. Tropical flowers flourished and bloomed in every corner, tumbling in abundance from urns. She hovered by the fountain, watching the water fall and spread a pattern of ripples across the surface while she struggled to get a grip on herself. Circe sidled out from beneath the foliage to brush against her legs, and she distractedly bent to stroke her elegant cat.

Before she'd married Raif, she had told herself that she would not get wound up about the fact that he loved another woman. And yet what was she doing right now? That question was unanswerable. She swallowed hard. Nahla had no idea of Raif's feelings, had evidently never once looked at Raif in a romantic light because he was younger than her and she had already been falling in love with the man she had married...and *lost*. Belatedly, it dawned on Claire that Nahla was a widow now and available, only Raif hadn't known that crucial fact until he'd returned to Quristan and by then he had already been married to Claire.

Had he railed at the cruel fate that had set him up with such bad timing that he'd lost out on a possible relationship with the woman he loved? Her tummy lurched at that acknowledgement. But nothing could be changed, she thought heavily. She was pregnant, the mother of the future Crown Prince. Raif was stuck with her as a wife whether he wanted to be or not. At this moment, neither of them had the freedom to make other choices and she had to woman up and face the emotional fallout of such a confession.

Certainly, she would not be blaming Raif for seeking out Nahla's company, she thought humourlessly. Raif had avoided the other woman to the best of his ability. No, Raif would not cheat on her. Raif was too honest and scrupulous for such behaviour. She reckoned that both of them were, never mind the fact that Nahla was still grieving for the husband she had loved.

'Claire...' Raif murmured quietly.

The woman I believed I was in love with for years.

His explanation sounded like a crack of doom in her memory and it wounded her like the short sharp shock of a lightning strike, knocking her right out of her happy place of security. And that was the terrible irony, she acknowledged unhappily. Raif *was* her happy place. From the day of their marriage, he had made her happy, so happy she could sometimes barely credit it, and yet right from the outset she had been fully aware that another woman had his heart. How naïve had she been not to appreciate that that horrible truth would eventually come back to haunt her?

'Claire...' Raif repeated, striding down the winding wrought-iron steps that led down from the sitting room into the court-yard. 'Much as I would prefer to avoid ever mentioning that name again, we have to talk about this.'

Claire avoided looking at him and studied his shadow instead. 'I can't think of much to say. That was what you might describe as a conversation killer,' she reasoned in a strained undertone.

'Did you even *listen* to what I actually said?' Raif chided. 'I said the woman that I *believed* I loved. It wasn't love, Claire. It was a teenage crush, which I assumed was love. And that assumption made me feel much more normal mixing with my peers. I may not have been chasing girls with my friends, but I was not sexless.'

Claire wasn't listening as well as she should have been. 'She's very beautiful,' she remarked stiffly. 'And she's warm and kind. As a teenager, you had surprisingly good taste.'

'But unhappily for me, I decided I was in love before I even understood what love was. I was a romantic, an idealist,' he breathed ruefully. 'A young woman who was out of reach…being almost a family member…was a safe focus for those feelings. She was in love with someone else and soon to be married. There was never the smallest prospect of anything of a romantic nature developing between us.'

Claire emerged from her reverie of unhappy thoughts and her brow furrowed as she turned back to him. 'You're saying it wasn't *real* love.'

'It felt real to me because I had no other woman to focus on and, let us be frank, the way I lived before I met you, that was enough for me to feel at the time. My mother's lifestyle had sickened me. Loving cleanly from afar suited me and gave me yet another reason to reject casual sex and relationships,' he proffered. 'Hell, Claire…

have you any idea how foolish I feel trying to explain this all to you now?'

Claire lifted her head, her blue eyes wary. 'Why would you feel foolish?'

'Because I was the idiot who thought an innocent crush was everlasting love!' Raif bit out with scorn. 'Even though I never lusted after her, even though I never made any attempt to see more of her, I still didn't understand my own feelings enough to re-alise that it was nothing more than an in-nocent boy's infatuation! But I should have seen the difference.'

'Let's go back upstairs,' Claire urged, fearful of them being overheard, already having espied a maid in the hall doorway, the woman clearly wondering if she should offer to serve them refreshments.

Claire started up the staircase in the wake of Circe, struggling to grasp what Raif was telling her. That he didn't love Nahla, after all? Was that what he was saying? Or was she only hearing what she wanted to hear? Mistakenly interpreting his words to mean what she wanted them to mean? Her brain was whirling with disconnected thoughts and her emotions were running on high. She simply couldn't think clearly.

At the top of the stairs, she moved into the sitting room, where Circe jumped on an armchair and curled up in graceful cat relaxation. 'I'm sorry I took off like that.'

'You're still not listening,' Raif censured, poised and deadly serious.

'You're saying it wasn't love,' she responded, disconcerting him with that quiet analysis. 'When did you decide that?'

'About the same time that I finally realised that I was in love with my wife. That was my true wake-up call. But, unluckily, I'd already shot myself in the foot by telling you that I was in love with someone else.' Raif sighed.

Claire blinked rapidly, not quite believing what she had heard, and she stared at him. 'What on earth are you talking about? We're talking in circles and you're confusing me.'

A groan of frustration fell from Raif's lips. 'You don't believe me, which is why I didn't try to tell you sooner. I went about this all the wrong way.'

He had realised that he was in love with his wife? But that was *her*! Claire gazed back at him, captured by stunning dark golden eyes and the increasing tension in his stance. He couldn't mean that, he couldn't possibly mean that!

'When did you realise that? That you thought you might…love me?' she queried unevenly.

'It was many weeks ago, but I should have recognised my feelings sooner. From the moment I met you, I could think of nothing *but* you! From that day, I was consumed by my thoughts and my memories of you. Doesn't it occur to you that my behaviour with you when we met was wildly out of character? I should have been the least likely man in the world to have a random one-night stand,' he pointed out. 'But you broke through my defences, and it was as though you cast a spell over me because, after you, nothing else mattered.'

'You walked away, afterwards,' Claire objected, because that still rankled and stung.

'And I pined for weeks on the yacht like a blasted schoolboy!' Raif complained. 'But I didn't think I had anything more to offer you because I still believed that I loved Nahla and I didn't want to drag you into some grubby affair that had nowhere to go.'

'You *pined*?' Claire pressed in disbelief.

'I pined. I wouldn't let myself phone or text you and I told myself that a clean break was the best I could offer you.'

'Oh, thanks for that,' Claire quipped, tongue in cheek.

'You deserved more from me, and I knew it,' Raif told her squarely.

'And then you discovered that I was on your yacht,' Claire continued.

Yet the whole time they were talking, her mind was racing ahead. He had said that he loved her. Raif had said that he loved her. She wanted to jump up and down, throw champagne, toss balloons and entire flocks of doves into the blue sky. The man she loved *loved* her right back and that was more than she had ever hoped to have.

'That was a shock. All those weeks I had been thinking about you, you were within reach…but yet *not* because I could not have renewed our relationship while you worked for me,' he asserted tautly. 'Yet I would have wanted to, so I'm grateful that we weren't faced with that temptation.'

'I spent almost half the trip worrying that I was pregnant.'

'I deeply regret that you went through those weeks of anxiety without my support.' His dark golden eyes were glittering like polished ingots in the sunshine flooding through the windows. 'But, let me say this only once…our son is a gift and a blessing. We are very fortunate.'

And Raif truly meant those sentiments, Claire registered with her eyes stinging a little from over-emotional tears. When it came to her pregnancy, Raif daily demonstrated his commitment to them both and he studied every ultrasound image with fascination and pleasure. He had not missed out on a single one of her health check-ups either. Her medical care was incredibly good, with the obstetrician coming to the palace to see her every week.

'You've got no resentment about our baby and the timing at all?'

'The most important thing our son achieved was to bring you back to me,' Raif asserted with a brilliant smile. 'You've turned my whole life around.'

'Well…' Claire murmured, crossing the

floor to slide her hand meaningfully into his. 'You gave me a palace to live in, a state-of-the-art kitchen and a great deal of happiness.'

Claire urged him gently in the direction of their bedroom, leaving Shahbaz to work out for himself that there was no point offering them coffee.

'I like watching you dance in the kitchen,' he confided.

Claire flushed and turned to close the door behind them. 'I didn't know you'd seen that.'

'Sometimes I spy on you. I didn't mention it because I don't ever want you to stop dancing,' Raif confessed. 'So you believe me about Nahla?'

Claire wrinkled her nose. 'I'm not sure I understand why you're uncomfortable when she's around—'

'Which of us enjoy being reminded of our teenage misapprehensions?' Raif traded wryly. 'But I'll get over it. Some day I'll look back on that piece of stupidity and laugh, but I cannot laugh at anything that threatens to divide us. I would have been wiser never to

mention her at all than to make such a production out of it.'

'No. I appreciated your honesty at the
time and I appreciate it now...more than you
know,' Claire told him gently as she unknot-
ted his tie and cast it aside. 'But the truth is
that I love you to death and even if you *still*
thought you loved her, I'd still love you to
death because you're a very special man.'

'You love me? Even though I spoiled our
marriage from the outset with that stupid
confession of mine about Nahla?' Raif questioned incredulously. 'I wanted to tell you
weeks ago that I loved you, but I felt that
I couldn't because, after what I'd told you
about Nahla, you'd never have believed me.'

'I'm believing you now,' Claire pointed
out, embarking on his shirt buttons. 'Love
shows in so many things you've done for
me. If I'd had stronger self-esteem, I would
have worked out that you loved me a long
time ago, but I was never going to tell you
that I loved you when I thought you loved
someone else.'

'I take it the Nahla business is behind us
now.' Able to take a hint, Raif doffed his
jacket and shed his shirt. 'I can't credit that

you fell in love with me too. When did that start?'

'That very first night,' Claire admitted, rather misty-eyed.

'I like that,' Raif admitted as he swept her dress up over her head. 'I suppose that's when I started developing feelings too. I didn't want to leave you and I wanted to turn time back and have that night over again. I love you so much. I had no idea that it was even possible to love anyone as much as I love you.'

Claire peeled off her remaining garments and lay back on the bed to watch him strip. 'I still get a kick out of watching you strip,' she confessed.

'Any time...' Raif promised, making a production out of getting down to his bare skin.

Claire laughed as he came down to her on the bed, lean, muscular and golden in the sunshine lighting up the room.

'I will never stop wanting you,' he told her urgently as he claimed a passionate kiss and the silence crept in around them slowly, punctuated only with the occasional moan or sigh. They made love with the urgency of two people who both felt as if they might have missed out on each other. Even so, they had made it through all the misunderstandings and their mutual happiness was so strong they sat up talking and loving half the night. There were no more secrets, no more doubts or insecurities between them.

'Go to sleep,' Raif urged her tenderly around dawn. 'I love you so much.'

'I love you too,' she whispered drowsily. 'But I don't want jungle animals in the nursery, just elephants because some animals are scary.'

'One little tiger hiding in the undergrowth of a jungle wall mural? It's the art of compromise,' Raif bargained, folding her into his arms and drifting off to sleep.

EPILOGUE

Ten years later

CLAIRE TUCKED IN the littlest and latest occupant of the royal nursery. Zakar was six months old, a cheerful baby with an untidy shock of black hair, who slept like a dream. The jungle wall in the nursery, painted by a Quristani artist, still featured a tiger cub below a tree, although Circe and her Siamese partner, Ninja, had acquired a spot as well, posed with regal cool nearby, with kittens round their feet, seemingly unperturbed by the elephants bathing in the river below them.

Claire smiled ruefully, thinking about her eldest, Rohaan, who had regularly disturbed her nights. He was now a lively, highly intelligent nine-year-old, and he still required less sleep than their other children. Her second pregnancy had been a twin one, and her little girls, Salima and Madiya, had arrived a few weeks early and demanded enough attention to ensure that two nannies were added to the staff. Zakar would be their last child, because Claire felt that four children was a nice round number, particularly now that they had two boys and two girls. She knew, though, that Raif, who adored babies, would probably eventually try to change her mind.

In the years that had passed since their marriage, Claire had gained poise. She had grown into her royal role and had learned that just being herself covered most occasions. She had picked up the language year on year and no longer needed an interpreter at her elbow. Nahla had fallen madly in love with one of Kashif's friends in the diplomatic corps and, having remarried, was now based in London. Claire missed the brunette, but Stella had become a close friend after Kashif was moved back to Quristan and settled into a more senior position in Kazan. As they now had three children, the two couples socialised a lot together.

Her brother, Tom, was a regular visitor and she always saw him when they stopped over in London. Sarah, her stepmother, had, sadly, passed away from an undetected heart condition, which was why she and Tom made an extra effort to spend time together because they were all that remained of their original family.

Circe, still famous from her glory days as a cartoon cat, had a chain of descendants now from her alliance with Ninja, the pedigreed Siamese given to Claire by Raif on the occasion of their first anniversary. They had kept two of their kittens, Ra and Bastet, who were very attached to the children.

Right now, as Claire tucked in her youngest son, Raif joined her, pausing only to smooth a light hand over his son's untidy head. 'All set?' he checked.

'I feel so guilty leaving the kids behind,' Claire admitted ruefully.

'They'll have a whale of a time with Kashif and Stella. Our kids get loads of holidays,' Raif reminded her. 'This is a special anniversary. Ten years since the first day we met.'

It was true that their children enjoyed plentiful away time from the royal household, Claire conceded. There were bucket-and-spade holidays in the old castle at Rabalissa, Mediterranean trips on the yacht and sometimes visits to their villa in the Alpujarra.

And that evening as they walked up the path from the cove to the little cottage where they had spent their very first night together, both of them were awash with fond memories.

'I should make you do a strip in the cove first,' Claire teased him.

'Only after dark and with company,' Raif declared with a wicked grin. 'But I'm not planning to let you outdoors any time soon, *aziz*.'

Claire laughed. Unlike most women, she got to celebrate two anniversaries every year, the anniversary of their first meeting and the anniversary of their marriage. It was so strange to walk into the little house where she had spent all those months with her late mother. Raif had bought it as a surprise for her the previous Christmas and had it renovated, so, although there was a haunting familiarity to the rooms, there was also a much greater level of comfort.

Raif leant up against the bedroom door and then straightened to remove his jacket very slowly. 'Do you still think I'm beautiful?' he asked her teasingly.

'Yes, and I'm a hopelessly shallow woman who worships you for your body alone,' she teased back.

He captured her face between his big

hands and kissed her with passionate fervour. 'I love you so much, Claire. I love you more with every passing year.'

'I love you too,' she whispered with the same adoring intensity, the strength of their love deepened by all that they had shared.

They didn't make it down to the cove until after midnight and Mohsin kept the security team at a safe distance. Owing to Raif's conviction that they had to do everything the same way as they had that first night, Claire conceived a fifth and final time and their youngest son, little Raza, was born nine months later.

* * * * *

If you fell in love with
The Baby the Desert King Must Claim
then you're sure to love these other stories by Lynne Graham!

Her Best Kept Royal Secret
Promoted to the Greek's Wife
The Heirs His Housekeeper Carried
The King's Christmas Heir
The Italian's Bride Worth Billions

Available now!